A FUNNY KIND OF MAN HATER

Sally Shore wore a man's peacoat, a sea captain's cap, and a manner that signaled loud and clear that she wanted no other part of a man.

Until now, at least.

Now she was in Ruff Justice's cabin, without a stitch of any kind of clothing on her voluptuous body.

"All that touching and kissing and poking you're always doing with that girl, Nancy Hawkins—have you got a little of it for me, tall man?"

Her lips parted when Ruff's mouth met hers. First she stroked his long dark hair, and then reached down to his legs as Ruff's lips roved across her breasts.

It soon became clear to Ruff that Sally didn't want just a little—she wanted a lot. . . .

RUFF JUSTICE #18

THE RIVERBOAT QUEEN

by

Warren T. Longtree

A SIGNET BOOK
NEW AMERICAN LIBRARY

PUBLISHER'S NOTE

This novel is a work of fiction. Names, characters, places, and incidents either are the product of the author's imagination or are used fictitiously, and any resemblance to actual persons, living or dead, events, or locales is entirely coincidental.

NAL BOOKS ARE AVAILABLE AT QUANTITY DISCOUNTS WHEN USED TO PROMOTE PRODUCTS OR SERVICES. FOR INFORMATION PLEASE WRITE TO PREMIUM MARKETING DIVISION, NEW AMERICAN LIBRARY, 1633 BROADWAY, NEW YORK, NEW YORK 10019.

The first chapter of this book appeared in *Drum Roll*, the seventeenth volume of this series.

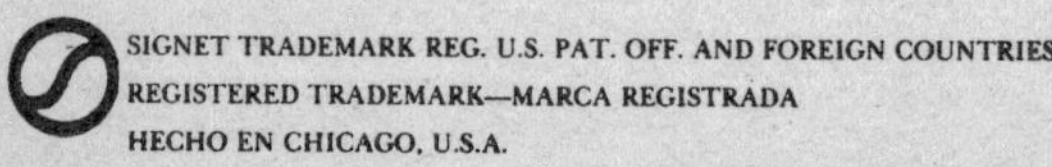

SIGNET, SIGNET CLASSIC, MENTOR, PLUME, MERIDIAN AND NAL BOOKS are published by New American Library,
1633 Broadway, New York, New York 10019

First Printing, February, 1985

1 2 3 4 5 6 7 8 9

PRINTED IN THE UNITED STATES OF AMERICA

RUFF JUSTICE

He knew the West better than any man alive—a hostile, savage land rife with both violent outlaws and courageous adventurers. But Ruff Justice had a sixth sense that kept him breathing and saw his enemies dead. A scout for the U.S. Cavalry, he was paid to protect the public, and nobody was faster at sniffing out a killer, a crook, a con man—red or white, at close range or far. Anyone on the wrong side of the law would have to reckon with the menace of Ruff's murderously sharp stag-handled bowie knife, with his Colt pistol, and the Spencer rifle he cradled in his arms.

Ruff Justice, gentleman and frontier philosopher—good men respected him, bad men feared him, and women, good and bad, wanted him with all the wildness of the Old West.

1

She could have been a dancer. She had the moves, the grace, the physical determination, the raw beauty. But it was fortunate for Ruff Justice that she wasn't a dancer. All of that splendid natural talent had been put to other uses, and Ruth Dawkens was really quite good at what she did.

She sat facing him, straddling his hips, her long blond hair cascading across her pale, smooth shoulders in a silvery torrent. Her breasts were full, high, pink-budded, smooth beneath the hands of Mr. Justice, the civilian scout working under Col. MacEnroe at Fort Lincoln, Dakota Territory.

Mr. Justice was no dancer. It would have been a waste of time to try to teach him, but he too, it seemed, had his raw physical talent. At least Ruth Dawkens thought so, and no one had proved her a liar.

The woman with the warmly lighted eyes bent low and kissed Ruff Justice on the lips and eyes before sitting up again, letting her finger trail along the line of his long dark mustache, which drooped now past his jawline, framing a slightly mocking mouth.

"I wish I didn't have to leave," Ruth said.

"You don't." Ruff's hands reached behind the woman and gripped her smooth, ivory-white buttocks, feeling the strength beneath the soft, feminine layer of flesh. She quivered slightly and smiled.

"Yes, I do, Ruff. There's nothing for me here, and you know it."

"There's me."

She made a small contented sound and leaned forward to kiss him again. "I know that, but you'll be going back to work soon too. The colonel isn't going to want this sick leave going on forever."

"No." Ruff frowned slightly at the thought of MacEnroe.

"Since there's never been any word about Marcia . . ." She fell silent, thinking about her sister, her lost sister who had run off with a renegade Indian. "Well" —she shrugged—"we knew it had to end."

"Not today," he said, his hands running up her arms to her shoulders.

"No, not today." She lay against him and her hips lifted and rolled to one side slightly, a small movement that inflamed Ruff Justice. His fingers trailed down the knuckles of her spine to the cleft of her ass. She sighed contentedly and snuggled against him, her pelvis nudging his, rising and falling.

Ruff felt her hand reach back and find him; her fingers encouraged him, stroking, gripping fingers, grown familiar now—familiar, competent, and eager: a dancer's fingers.

"I don't want to go," Ruth said. Her words were muffled. She spoke against his chest, her dancer's body beginning to speed its rhythm, its thrust, as her inner muscles worked against Justice.

"I know."

"Don't want to . . ." She puffed. "But I have to."

Ruth sat up and leaned her head back, her lips parted, her eyes half-closed as she slowly raised and lowered herself on Ruff's shaft. Justice watched her, liking the concentration on her face, the distant pleasure in her eyes, the cascade of silver hair, the rising and falling breasts, ripe and round, the patch of soft down, the heat of her body, the sleek strength of her thighs, the length of her calves rounded with firm muscle, the small feet.

She lifted herself higher yet and then settled with a deep sigh, finishing with a series of tiny, jerking movements, her body growing wet, heavy, as she sagged forward unsteadily against Ruff, who had found his own rhythm and now lifted her with the action of his body, spreading her wider with his searching fingers, hearing her breathing in his ear, the urging, meaningless little words, before he spilled himself in Ruth and lay back to clutch at her, to touch and fondle, to feel her sweet breath and searching lips on his face, throat, and chest.

The door banged open and the woman just barged in.

She was tall and angular and raucous with a blue peacoat on her back, a mop of sawed-off red hair spilling out from under a sea captain's hat.

"Just about what I figured—I know men," she said.

"Good," Ruff Justice said mildly. "Then you know what I'm going to do to you if you don't turn around and get out of here, woman."

"All talk. Just like 'em all. Get up, boy. You are Ruffin T. Justice, aren't you? Your colonel's got a job for you. Namely, working for me."

"Colonel MacEnroe sent you here!" Ruff sputtered a little. He and the colonel had their share of run-ins, but this didn't seem like MacEnroe's tactics.

"Ah, hell no. He gave me some malarkey about you being on sick leave or some such. I said to myself if he's like any man I ever knew he's sick with a blonde beside him."

Ruff slowly sat up, Ruth rolling to one side to draw her knees up and tug the sheet up under her chin. They could only stare at the big redheaded woman. Big she was, but not fat, and not so old as Ruff had first imagined. Middle twenties, perhaps.

"Well, let's get up. I told the colonel I couldn't

hardly get my work done while the man who was *supposedly* going to help me was frolickin' in the sack."

"Look, Miss . . ."

"Shore. I'm Sally Shore, you probably heard of me, everyone has."

Ruff hadn't, but she didn't give him time to say so. She went on, "The colonel wouldn't tell me where you were, so I stormed out of there. It didn't take much to find this cozy port, though. A hotel, I figured; then I give the desk clerk a spot of silver money and he sent me up." She had her hands on her hips. "So . . . here I am, there you are. Get up and let's get together!"

For a minute Ruff thought she was going to reach down and flip the sheet back, but she restrained herself. He took a deep breath before he let himself respond.

"Sally Shore, I want you to turn around and get out of here. I mean, right now. I don't know what your business is and I don't care."

"The army—"

"The army's given me some time off. When they need me back, they'll let me know in some slightly more discreet manner. I don't know if you're dumb or just all brass, but I'd appreciate it if you'd back into the hall and think it over."

Sally Shore just stared at him, her tongue pushing at the inside of her cheek. She winked.

She just winked, turned around, and with her hands thrust in her coat pockets, she sauntered out into the hallway, closing the door sharply behind her.

"What," Ruth said, laughing, "was that?"

Justice had no answer for her. It beat all. The woman was plain audacious. Ruff got up. He sat on the edge of the bed, rubbing his head for a minute.

"What are you going to do?" Ruth asked, her hand on his back.

"See what she wants. If I don't, she'll be back."

From the hallway Sally Shore called out, "You're damned right I'll be back, Ruffin T. Justice!"

Ruth laughed. Ruff shook his head and got up from the bed, crossing the room to where his clothes lay on the chair—his buckskin pants and buckskin shirt, white hat. His gun belt rested on one post of the chair.

Ruth, yawning, also rose.

"I thought maybe you'd wait here," Ruff said.

"Can't, Mister Justice." She put her arms around his waist, rested her head on his chest. "I've got to see about a ticket east."

"You're seriously going?" He tilted her chin up.

"I'm seriously going," she said. There was just a little moisture gathering in the corners of her deep-brown eyes. Ruff kissed the top of her head.

"I'll be back later. We'll make it a fine good-bye," he promised. He had started toward the door before she replied.

"All right. Ruffin . . ." He looked back expectantly, but she just shook her head and turned away.

Ruff stood silently for a moment, watching her bare back. Then he went out to deal with Sally Shore.

She was leaning against the wall in the corridor, one foot propped up behind her. Her hat was tilted rakishly on her dark-red hair.

"Through? I thought maybe you'd pause for another helping."

"What do you want?" Justice asked. He hadn't quite warmed to the woman and she wasn't helping matters any.

"Told you what I wanted. Colonel says you're my helper. Let's get going."

"Lady, you're just a little pushy."

"Yeah. I know. That's what got me where I am." She came away from the wall. "You ready?"

"No. I have to talk to the colonel before I do anything."

"Just red tape. I'll tell you all you need to know."

Justice wasn't listening. He was walking down the corridor toward the hotel stairs, wondering how a day that began so promisingly could have turned sour so quickly.

He managed to recover his gray horse from the stable and ride out of Bismarck toward the fort without Sally Shore on his tail, but he met her again inside the colonel's office. She wasn't going to be easy to shake, it seemed.

"Hello, Ruff," Colonel MacEnroe said from behind his desk. He was a hard man with clean features, a silver mustache, and the air of authority. Just now he looked a little bedazzled. "You've met Miss Shore?"

"Yes," Justice said. He took a corner chair and sat down, crossing his long legs, balancing his hat on his knee. Sally Shore yawned broadly.

"Sorry, Ruff. How's the leg, by the way?" Justice had been nicked by a bullet, the cause of his sick leave, which Sally Shore had so rudely and abruptly ended.

"It's fine now, sir."

"Apparently the man's in working order from one end to the other," Sally Shore said. "So let's skip 'How's your ma and how's your pa,' and get down to brass tacks."

MacEnroe's face paled just a little and the muscles at the hinge of his jaw twitched, but he didn't respond. Instead, he turned to Justice.

"As you know, Ruffin, the Sioux are kicking up their heels to the northwest. We're having a hell of a time supplying Fort Benton overland. The freighters won't even try it anymore. Miss Shore is going to have a go at it."

"She's a teamster?"

"Steamboat captain." The colonel held up his hand as Ruff started to object automatically. "I know, I know—it's a bad stretch of water from here to the Marias. Shallow some places, quick in others. No steamboat has ever tried to get that far up the

Missouri, but Miss Shore has a shallow draft vessel that she is convinced can make it through to Benton, and, Justice, we have to take the chance. Regiment has made the decision already."

"The Sioux will never let her get through. Aside from that, Jack Troll and his thugs control the river from here to Fort Union. Benton is four hundred land miles from Lincoln; the river route makes it half again as long."

"I know that, Ruff," the colonel said, "but the men at Benton need food, ammunition, tools to complete that fort by winter. They're virtually cut off, besieged by the Sioux. This is a long chance, but it's about the only one we have."

Ruff Justice felt his mouth tighten. He didn't like any part of this idea. If regiment didn't know the upper Missouri, he did. It was a wild, unpredictable thing. He had rapids and falls and hostile Indians ahead of him, river bandits and hard weather.

And worst of all, he had Miss Sally Shore to deal with. He looked again at the smug, overconfident redheaded woman, and then shrugged.

"All right. I'll have at it, Colonel. All I need is a little time for a few good-byes."

2

Ruff walked along the dockside plank walk, looking out across the glittering Missouri River, amazed at the clutter of boats that ran the river these days.

Not long ago you saw nothing but an occasional birchbark and now and again a flatboat loaded with back-country furs drifting toward Omaha or St. Louis. Now the river had discovered steam, and there were twenty or thirty power-driven boats at the Bismarck dock, the majority of them bringing building and food supplies upriver: bricks and cement, canned goods, flour, sugar, and molasses. They returned with loads of hides or furs, some wheat from the farms that were beginning to transform the wild plains into wheat country, and a few brokenhearted passengers, women mostly, who had come West and busted.

But Bismarck had always been the upper end of the river until now. Going farther upstream was considered suicidal. Sally Shore, whoever or whatever she was, had different ideas.

Ruff Justice put his pack down and stood, sheathed rifle in hand, watching the loading of the sternwheeler, the *Jacksonville*.

The boat was Sally Shore's boat, and it was bigger, brighter, and newer than Ruff had expected. White with black and dark-green trim, it had two fancy, flared stacks that were dribbling a little dark smoke into the pale silvery sky.

Sally Shore claimed she drew only five feet of water. Ruff reckoned that might prove to be about four feet too many for the Upper Mo. He hoped it was raining upcountry; they would need all the help they could get.

He started on. The laborers carrying an assortment of supplies for Fort Benton walked narrow, bowing planks in a trudging single file. On the upper deck of the steamboat someone who might have been Sally Shore leaned out, turned her head away, and shouted an order.

A thick-armed man wearing a rolled-up white shirt and a blue cap stood watching Ruff's approach from the dock beside the *Jacksonville.*

"You Ruffin T. Justice?" the big man asked, making it sound very amusing.

"That's right?" Justice answered with sun-narrowed eyes.

"Come on, then, I'll show you your cabin." He looked Ruff up and down again, smiled to himself, and led the way up a bow gangplank.

Ruff followed, wondering what in hell it is that makes people disdain anything they aren't. A sailor has contempt for anyone who doesn't sail; onshore they mock the seaman.

He stepped over the rail and followed the man along the deck beside the brightly painted wheelhouse. The way was crowded with men carrying molasses barrels, with the returning, empty-handed laborers, with sailors toting heavy lines or nameless gear.

"This one," the sailor leading Ruff said. He toed open the wooden cabin door and Justice went in. "It'll do, I take it?" The mockery was bright and hard in the man's voice.

Justice looked the man over more closely. Square-faced, pale-eyed, he had a lugubrious mouth and a flattened, wide nose. "You got something against me, friend?" Justice asked.

"Why, we've never even met, have we?" the sailor answered, but there was a hint of a sneer in his words still.

The door opened again and Sally Shore fluttered in, her excited movements filling the cabin. She looked Justice up and down like a side of beef and offered what might have been a smile—a sort of crooked upside-down frown.

"You two met?" she asked, nodding to the sailor.

"Not exactly," Ruff said. He tossed his gear on the bunk and placed his rifle in the corner.

"This is Lydell Cherry, my first."

"First what?"

"Mate," Sally Shore said impatiently. Ruff could still recall his own first mate, and she was a lot prettier than Lydell Cherry, who stood glowering. "Lydell, this is Ruffin Justice. The army's sent him along to guide us upriver."

"I know who he is." Lydell turned his head and deliberately spat. Then he spun away and walked out of the cabin, banging the door behind him. Dust danced in the ribbons of light that fell through the slats in the cabin door. Ruff watched them for a time until Sally said, "Well."

She scratched at her mop of red hair and planted her captain's hat again. "What did you rub his nose in, Justice?"

"Never saw him before now," Justice said honestly.

"Funny. Cherry's a little quirky now and then, but this ain't like him." Her expression changed, the tone of her voice softened but became more challenging at the same time. "Get your good-byes all said, did you?"

"That's right." And Ruth Dawkens was at the stage depot, going East. He would never see her again, and it was a shame.

"Good. Want to look around the boat?"

"Sure." He offered her a smile, which she didn't respond to. Ruff guessed there was nothing amusing about the *Jacksonville.* They went out of the cabin and strolled the lower deck, where the loading was taking place. Well, at least Ruff strolled, being in no hurry. Sally yanked at his arm, screeched at the laborers, called orders up to the pilot on the upper deck, broke into a rather masculine stream of curses, and ignored him in turn.

He saw the cargo area—abovedecks on a shallow riverboat—looked over the stern at the big paddle wheel, went to the engine room, studied the boilers and the mass of steam pipes like interwound snakes. On the upper deck there was a salon of sorts; Sally tersely explained, "Used to run passengers. The women liked their fancy ways."

"And the men liked the fancy women," Ruff added.

Sally looked at Ruff, her mouth going tight with an emotion he couldn't peg. "Yeah," she said, "that's why I went to cargo. Run cotton, it don't throw other bales of cotton overboard, don't get drunk and bother the pilot, don't start shooting after a bad draw in five-card—"

"I get the idea."

"Yeah. People are trouble. Male people are worse than that."

Ruff wondered silently who the man had been that had strangled Sally Shore's heart. He said nothing, following her to the wheelhouse, where a cheerful, white-whiskered man in a blue suit with gold buttons sat smoking a pipe. He rose from his chair and crossed the wheelhouse, touching the huge wooden wheel in passing in an almost superstitious gesture.

"This is Cap MacAdoo. Used to have his own side-wheeler, but she busted up. I was lucky enough to get him. He's my pilot, and the best on the river—on any river."

Justice stuck out his hand and the little man took it

warmly, beaming as if he'd found a long lost son. "How do you do," Cap said.

"This is Ruff Justice," Sally said as if she'd lost interest in him.

"I hear it's plenty rough upriver," Cap said around his pipe stem.

"It's rough. No one's ever tried it before, you know. Not above Fort Union," Ruff answered.

"Well, we'll give it our best try."

"Try, hell," Sally Shore said, "we're going through with the goods. Got to," she added to herself just loudly enough for Ruff to hear, though he thought she hadn't meant him to. "Come on, Justice. I got work to do."

Outside, the loading went on. The Missouri stretched away endlessly in a broad silver band. A half-unloaded freight wagon stood near the gangplank and a knot of men moved around in confusion.

A sailor in the red-striped shirt shouted up to Sally. "They've got the wrong shipment, Miss Shore!"

"Who is it?" she hollered back.

"Granger and Sample."

"Christ," she muttered, "how do those idiots stay in business? I'm coming down." She asked Ruff, "Can you get along on your own?"

"I have for a number of years now."

"Yeah." Sally headed for the dock, leaving Ruff to lean against the rail and watch Bismarck, the fort, the river, and the long skies.

In a minute he saw Sally walk purposely down the gangway and onto the dock, where she tangled with a teamster about twice her size, giving him hell about the shipment.

Ruff watched it until it ceased to be diverting, then he wandered around to the other side of the boat and down to the cabin deck. He passed Lydell Cherry and got a dark look. Ruff searched his memory for Cherry, for anyone with that name, but came up with nothing. He shrugged it off. Some people just didn't seem to take to him. The first mate was apparently one of these.

Ruff returned to dockside and found the loading had dwindled. Sailors stood around the rail watching their boss berate the teamster, who only shook his head dumbly and continued to try to show Sally a piece of paper.

"I don't care what it says there . . ." Ruff ceased listening and yawned broadly.

"Justice!" Sally Shore called. "Say, Justice!"

He looked over and saw Sally waving her arm in a wide arc. He started down. She was still arguing with the stubborn teamster when he got there.

"Look, I've got to get this mess straightened out," Sally told him. "Someone has to go over to Fletcher's and find out what's holding up the lumber. You know where it is, don't you?"

"Yes." Ruff was smiling faintly. Sally had adopted him into her crew readily enough.

"You get over there and find Old Man Fletcher. Tell him I'm not waiting until tomorrow. I'd send my boys, but they don't know the town. Besides, you send a sailor past a saloon and you're asking for trouble. I know my sailors."

"You know men," Ruff prodded gently.

"That's right, I do! Look here, Justice—"

The weary teamster interrupted, "Lady, please! I got another delivery way out at the Big Oak Ranch."

"*Another* delivery. You haven't made this one yet. This ain't what I ordered—Justice get going, will you?—I told Sample precisely what was on the army requisition . . ."

Justice walked away from the boat. It was a warm day—Bismarck quiet, as it generally was in the middle of the week. There weren't many idlers around this town. It took money to be idle, and you had to work to make money. It made a nice circle and kept the streets relatively empty.

Ruffin waved to Johnny Peabody, who ran the

Country Diner, and walked up Third Street past the millinery shop, where a young lady in blue gave him an enticing backward glance.

Fletcher's Lumber Yard was at the end of the street. Ruff had known Fletcher for quite a while. The man had rolled into Bismarck with a steam engine and a saw blade, asked where the nearest supply of lumber was, and gotten to work. The logs had to roll a long way, and by the time Fletcher had finished his lumber, the cost was high, but there wasn't any other source for hundreds of miles. Fletcher did all right. He had the lumber yard and a two-story white house on the east end of town, and he was working on his second Indian wife. The first had run off because Fletcher refused to beat her.

Justice was two blocks from the lumber yard when he saw the injured man.

The low moans turned Ruff's head toward the narrow alley. He squinted into the deep shadows and saw the crumpled man lying there, writhing, holding his gut. Ruff turned that way sharply. He had gone ten feet when they hit him.

The man behind him had come from behind a rain barrel. As the man who had been faking injury reached for Ruff's ankles, the big man pinned his arms.

Ruff threw an elbow back and it landed solidly in the big man's ribs. He heard the muffled *oomph* beside his ear. Ruff reached for the big man's neck, intending to flip him, but the one on the ground had his feet now and Ruff was yanked to the earth and landed hard. There was a third one rushing toward them now, eager to be in on the kill.

Ruff's head rang from striking the ground, but he had presence of mind enough to kick the man in front of him in the face. He had started to rise; now he fell back again, blood seeping through his fingers. He didn't have to fake the pain this time.

The big man clung to Justice, digging massive fists

into his kidneys and ribs. Justice swung his skull back and the big man howled as his nose was broken. Blood gushed warmly from the shattered nose and Justice spun away, drawing his Colt.

The man who had been rushing to join the fray saw that big blue Colt come up, and he put on the brakes, being suddenly in as big a hurry to get out of that alley. Justice let one shot loose over the thug's head just to hurry him along.

When Ruff turned back, the other two were limping toward the head of the alley. He could have killed them. He could have chased them down. He just let them go.

"The hell with it." Some local thugs trying to pick up a little drinking money. Maybe they wouldn't have that idea again for a while.

Ruff holstered his Colt and wiped back his long dark hair. When he bent over to pick up his trampled stetson, he found a sap.

It was an odd-looking thing: a chunk of lead bound in twine, knotted intricately to form a sack for the weight. Ruff frowned over that little item. It had taken some time to make and it had been made by someone who knew knots intimately. Like a sailor.

He was glad they hadn't had a chance to use it. Ruff tossed it away and started toward the lumber yard, trying not to think of reasons why a sailor would want him dead.

It didn't take much to size up the lumber problem: Fletcher's big wagon had been broken down. They were just putting the new axle on when Ruff wandered in. Old Man Fletcher himself was there, waving his hands excitedly, speaking to the heavenly skies beyond the roof of his mill, which smelled of freshly sawn lumber, pine pitch, and scorched steel. He promised the lumber in an hour, and Ruff sat down to wait.

He rode back on the high wagon sitting beside the Chinese driver. Sally Shore was waiting on the dock when they got there. She didn't have time to thank Ruff Justice and he didn't have time to worry about it.

He was thinking about looking for something to eat when the little fringed surrey pulled up and a young lady with the chestnut curls got down.

She wore green satin and a tiny green hat with black lace on it. She was helped out of the surrey by a man wearing a cavalry uniform. The rank was major. He was tall, well-set-up, with a dark-brown mustache that jutted out in points, and a solid-looking jaw.

The other soldier was only a kid, wearing a second lieutenant's bars as if they were awkward weights on his narrow shoulders. He stood by, ungainly, angular, as the girl was handed down. She took the major's arm and they walked toward the gangway, the lieutenant following.

Ruff Justice knew none of them. That didn't stop him from trying. He managed to reach the gangplank just as the small party did.

"Pardon me," the major said in a way that wasn't so much begging pardon as telling Ruff to get the hell out of his way.

Justice was busy looking into a pair of remarkably wide, clear amber-colored eyes.

The owner of them blinked long lashes at him and cocked her head curiously. "Hello," she said, making it a question.

"I'm Ruff Justice," the scout said with a little bow. He kissed her hand as the major, scowling, tried to tug her away. The girl was young enough to be flattered, young enough to blush.

"Nancy Hawkins," she gasped.

"This is not the way my daughter is introduced to young men," the major said. His face had paled a little. There were red spots burned into his cheekbones. "Nor are you the sort she is going to be introduced to while I live."

That was a little strong. Ruff smiled anyway. "Sorry, sir. I suppose my background is a little lacking. I didn't mean to offend you—or your lovely daughter." He backed away, and the major, somewhat mollified, huffed his way up the gangplank, the green lieutenant following hurriedly, his eyes straight ahead.

"And you tell me *I* don't have tact," Sally Shore said.

Ruff turned and shrugged. "Couldn't help myself."

"Yeah, I know. You're just a man. Hell of an excuse. How far do you think that'll carry you?"

Ruff looked up the gangway at the vanishing green satin bustle. "I don't know," he said thoughtfully. "I'd like to find out."

Sally made a disgusted noise in her throat and tramped away, shouting at the lumber-wagon driver.

Ruff went aboard the boat again and watched the hurried loading of the lumber, which would be used for finishing the inside walls of Fort Benton, for flooring and roofs, replacing the existing log and sod roof that dripped mud onto heads and desks, bunks and boots, with each rain.

Tar paper was being loaded and now crates of rifles and ammunition. The sacks of flour and salt were hastily unloaded from a low, flat wagon. It was like watching an anthill as men shouldered men moving up and down the gangplanks to the rear deck of the *Jacksonville.*

It actually didn't take that long. Within an hour they were putting the canvas tarps over the cargo, tying it down, and the docks were cleared of wagons.

"I ought to cut you down to size," the shaky voice said, and Ruff Justice turned toward the man with the bunched fists and pale face.

"Why's that, Lieutenant?" Ruff asked the young officer, who, trembling with rage, came forward a step, his lips compressed into a narrow bloodless line. A feathery wisp of pale hair fell out from under his hat, giving him a boyish look at odds with his warrior's stance.

"You insulted my fiancée," he said.

Ruff Justice pulled his silver watch from his pocket and snapped it open. He looked at it for a long minute and then put it away. "Took you long enough to work yourself up into this sweat, didn't it, Lieutenant?"

"I had to consider every side of this. I'm not one to rush into things."

"You haven't quite considered long enough," Ruff warned him, looking the kid over. "You're rushing into something you don't want here."

"I'm not afraid of you."

"Didn't think you were," Ruff said soothingly.

"Honor demands—"

"John! John Lewis Weeks!"

Both men turned as Nancy Hawkins, her chestnut ringlets bouncing like soft springs, scurried toward them, holding her dress off the deck.

"What are you doing? Did my father convince you to come up here and bother this man?"

Lt. Weeks hung his head automatically before remembering that he was a man and a warrior. "This is none of your business, Nancy," he said.

"Oh, yes, it is! You and father both. What's the matter with you? This man simply introduced himself to me. That is all there was to it." She inserted a quick smile at Ruff, which he accepted gravely. "The idea of fighting over such a thing is repugnant and childish."

"I was just getting ready to apologize, Miss Hawkins," Ruff Justice told her.

Weeks blinked at him in confusion, before he remembered again. "By God, I should hope you would apologize," Weeks said. It was probably, Ruff decided, a good imitation of Maj. Hawkins. When the lieutenant got a little older, he'd likely sport a long, pointed mustache.

Nancy Hawkins gave Ruff a grateful glance. She was a sharp one, Ruff decided, sharp and very pretty. She hooked her arm around Weeks' and prodded him with her elbow.

"Shake hands, please? For me, John. We've a long way to travel together. There's no sense in being enemies." She was speaking ostensibly to Weeks, but her eyes were on Ruff Justice.

Weeks stuck out a pink hand, and Ruff took it. The hand was soft and damp, but Weeks squeezed as hard as he could. Justice offered a token wince, and the young man seemed pleased enough. Then Ruff touched his hat brim to the lady, and she and Weeks walked away together, speaking in low rapid voices.

"Ain't young love grand?" Sally Shore said. She had come around the far side of the wheelhouse.

"How long have you been there?"

"Just long enough to see the end. Touching."

"Yes."

"We're casting off in five minutes."

"Good."

"You don't like this idea much, do you, Justice?" Sally said. She leaned beside him at the rail, her cap pushed back to let a wreath of red curls escape.

"What idea, Sally Shore?"

"You know—going upriver."

"Not much. The odds are too much against it. Sioux, river pirates, the Missouri itself."

"You're right." Ruff looked at her with surprise. "But it'll be done. One day, one way or another someone will do it. It might as well be me, now."

"You got a lot riding on this?" Ruff asked.

"All I have, tall man. The boat is in hock. It's liable to be a total loss if we hit a bad stretch of water."

"Why, then?"

"There's money to be made, Justice. If I make this run once, learn the channels, I'll be supplying that fort for years. Maybe Fort Union and Fort Peck as well with any luck. If I can prove I can do it, I can undercut those freighters by fifty percent and still get rich."

"That important to you?"

"It's important to everybody." A whistle tooted. "Cap's ready to shove off. Say, you ought to be nice to Major Hawkins; he's the new commander at Fort Benton, you know. He's liable to be your boss one day."

"Not if I can help it," Ruff muttered.

Sally laughed, lifted a hand, walked forward, her hips rolling, and shoved her hands in her back pockets.

Ruff went forward too to look ahead of the *Jacksonville* as the lines were cast off, the steam valves opened, the big stern wheel slowly beginning to revolve, pushing the big white boat out into the middle of the Missouri, her whistle tooting, kids running beside her along the wharf, waving and shouting, dogs yapping at their bare heels. Then the kids were left behind, and there was only the willow-lined Missouri. Ahead of them were six hundred miles of bad river.

Ruff turned and looked up to the wheelhouse, where the redheaded lady with the gall of six lumberjacks was steering the *Jacksonville.*

After a time Ruff returned to his cabin. Someone else had already been there. He couldn't tell what they had wanted, but they had been through his things. A small, limp object near the door caught his eye and Justice picked it up to examine it.

It was a sack made out of knotted twine.

If you put a chunk of lead in it, it would make a hell of a fine sap.

3

Ruff wore his dark suit, ruffled shirt, and dark hat to dinner. Inside the coat a Colt New Line .41 revolver rode in a shoulder holster that went with dining and cultured conversation a bit better than a belt gun.

The river was an endless, murmuring black thing, reptilian, hissing and muttering, flowing beneath the *Jacksonville* as she cut her way upstream in the night.

It had surprised Ruff that Sally Shore would risk running at night, but she meant to make as good a time as possible on the initial leg between Bismarck and Fort Mandan. She had told him that, and then she had surprised him even more by announcing, "We dine formal tonight. Seven o'clock. You be there." Then she had gone out, closing the cabin door sharply, leaving Ruff bemused. The woman had many sides, apparently.

In the darkness the trees along the shore were like so many black sentinels. Justice leaned out over the rail and watched the white water frothing past. The shadowy figure that appeared at his elbow caused him to draw back quickly.

"Sorry. Startle ya?" It was only Cap MacAdoo, his pipe thrust in his mouth, the glow from the bowl dimly lighting his white-whiskered face.

"Nerves are a little jumpy," Justice admitted.

"You?" Cap peered at Ruff, chuckling. "Man, I'd bet you got no nerves."

"You'd lose that bet." Justice noticed that Cap had a dark suit and stiff white shirt on. "You roped into the dinner too?"

"Yes. I don't know what's gotten into Sally now. She maybe wants to have a last bit of civilization before we leave it behind." Cap looked at the dark water, thinking silent thoughts for a minute. "The *Jacksonville* used to have some soirees on her in her time. Down South, that is. She used to come by lighted to the stacks, people drinking and dancing along the decks . . ." Cap shook his head.

"You had your own boat too, didn't you?"

"Oh, yes. You bet! More'n one, but the last one—that was the *Birmingham*—now, she was a boat. Put this one to shame, if you'll allow me some bragging."

"You were a passenger steamer too?"

"Yes. Mostly freight, but we had our share of to-dos in the ballroom."

"What happened to her?"

"The *Birmingham*?" Cap was silent in the night once more. Ruff heard him expel his breath between his teeth. "We hung her up on a bar—running at night in a storm. Ripped the bottom out of her. That was that." He spread his hands.

"Running at night?" Ruff said, looking to the wheelhouse.

"Just like us? Yes, but this is different. Visibility's good. Moon'll be up in an hour."

"Who's steering?"

"Cherry. He's a good-enough pilot."

"Cherry doesn't like me much. Any idea why?"

"Cherry don't need a reason. Lydell Cherry don't like anyone much."

That wasn't much of an explanation, but Ruff was willing to accept it for now.

Cap inclined his head and knocked out his pipe on the railing. "Coming? It must be close to seven."

"Sure." Ruff gestured with his hand and Cap started forward, Ruff beside and half a stride behind.

They were all there in the dining room when the two men arrived: Maj. Hawkins, stiff in his dress uniform; John Weeks, looking slightly flushed with wine, or manhood; Nancy Hawkins, turning toward Ruff with shining eyes, a glass in her hand refracting light from the chandelier overhead, her chestnut hair done up with pearls, her lavender gown clinging to the slopes and domes of her figure. And at the head of the linen-covered table, Sally Shore, looking uncomfortable but downright lovely in a dark dress, her red hair brushed if not arranged meticulously, a cut-crystal necklace around her throat, which was nut brown and, despite the powder she had used, faded rather dramatically to a smoothly pale cleavage.

She saw Ruff's eyes on her breasts and throat, started to snap something at him, then controlled herself and just turned her eyes away briefly. When they returned to him, they were placid, empty.

When Sally said seven, she apparently meant seven. They were invited to seat themselves according to the place markers, which had each name written on them. Sally, Ruff noted without surprise, had placed him at the other end of the table, as far from her as possible. The major looked slightly offended at not being offered a chair at the head of the table, but then, on board ship the captain was the person of highest rank.

Lt. Weeks was to Ruff's right, Nancy Hawkins to his left, then the major, facing Cap MacAdoo and Sally. A man in a white jacket came in and started serving.

"You look nice this evening," Nancy Hawkins said.

Weeks' head came up sharply from his soup.

"Thank you. I have been wanting to compliment you since I entered the room," Ruff Justice said. "I didn't wish to be forward. But since you have spoken to me, may I say that you are astonishingly beautiful as well as charming."

Weeks turned different colors and bit his tongue. He looked uncertainly at Ruff Justice, who sat erect in his dark suit, lace showing at the cuffs of his shirt. His dark hair was brushed to a gloss and his mustache neatly trimmed. Weeks' eyes slid away. He knew that there were currents in Justice he didn't understand. He was more than a little jealous, not mature enough to recognize or cope with the jealousy. He sipped his onion soup.

"There is no other solution," Maj. Hawkins was saying. "I'm hardly alone in my thinking. At different times Congressman Cavanaugh, General Sherman, and Colonel Chivington have all expressed the same opinion. I agree heartily with Cavanaugh's much-quoted remark, 'I have never seen a good Indian except when I have seen a dead one.' Yes, Miss Shore. They must be exterminated or driven from the United States."

"What do you think of the major's opinion, Mister Justice?" Lt. Weeks asked.

Ruff Justice lifted his eyes to the head of the table. His voice was very soft. "I think I've never heard such a criminal, irresponsible sack of vomit in my life. Please pass the rolls."

Maj. Hawkins body stiffened and his napkin balled in his hand. He pointed a trembling, stubby finger at Ruff Justice.

"The ones with the caraway seeds, please," Justice told the major.

"Are you in the employ of the United States Army, Mister Justice?" Hawkins demanded. His voice was quavering. It seemed to issue from deep within a cavern inside the man.

"Yes," Ruff said, "I am." He smiled at Nancy Hawkins. "It may be a rather temporary position. I seem to rub some people the wrong way. Butter, too, please."

Hawkins knew he was beat. He turned away. He didn't know how to handle people if they weren't susceptible to being browbeaten.

The meal was remarkably silent after that. Sally asked a few questions about life in the army and the major answered in monotone. Ruff enjoyed the meal, stuffed pork chops, corn-bread dressing, new potatoes, and carrots. He didn't have to interrupt his chewing to respond to anyone's conversation. No one seemed to want to talk to him.

After dinner they stood around drinking more wine. Ruff got tired of repeating that he didn't drink to the eager waiter and went outside to stand brooding by the rail.

"You did put it a little strongly," the voice beside him said, and he turned to find Nancy Hawkins, her face bright in the light of the rising moon, watching him.

"Did I? Mass slaughter has never ranked as one of my favorite topics."

"I thought you were an Indian fighter."

"I have fought Indians," Ruff said. Obviously he didn't want to continue the conversation along those lines, so Nancy let it dwindle away.

"Walk me around the deck?" she asked cheerfully.

"Won't your father mind—or Lieutenant Weeks?"

"Probably. I'm not a child, though. You're not afraid of them, are you?"

"I don't like trouble. A man has enough trouble trying to make it from the cradle to the grave."

"You don't like trouble," she repeated very soberly, and then they both laughed.

"Come on." She felt his arm slip around her and she let herself be guided along the deck. The night was cool, the moon golden and huge, gilding the river. Ruff asked, "You going to marry the lieutenant?"

"Is that what he told you?"

"Yes. Isn't it so?"

"I think he and Father have something like that planned. No one has discussed it with me." They had come to a wooden bench set beside the rail, and they sat down, Ruff's arm going around her shoulders.

"Why do you ask?" Nancy inquired.

"I'd like to know things like if a woman is married, planning on it, carries a gun strapped to her garter."

Nancy laughed. "No gun." She kissed him then, her fingers touching his jaw lightly. It was a sweet, girlish kiss, but there was heat behind it, barely restrained. It sent a ripple of want through Ruff's loins.

He bent forward, clasping his hands between his knees. The boat rounded a slow bend in the river. "What in the world are you doing going upriver on this boat?" he asked Nancy. "Is your father crazy?"

"Crazy?" Nancy stiffened a little. She looked at the tall man but saw no malice in his expression.

"It's dangerous, very dangerous," Ruff said.

"Why, it's perfectly lovely!" She gestured toward the moon-glossed river. A small laugh rose from her smooth throat.

"Here . . . now . . . but it's going to get hellish. If you didn't realize that, your father should have."

"I believe someone did say something about the river getting rather tricky."

"Did they say something about the Sioux being tricky just now?" Ruff asked with a shadow of sarcasm that he regretted. But damn the man! What was Hawkins thinking of bringing this girl along?

"I don't understand." The stiffness had returned. "My father is the new commanding officer at Fort Benton. He knew this steamboat was going upriver with supplies. He elected to travel aboard himself to see how the experiment works."

"And risk your life doing it." Ruff didn't expect an answer and didn't get one. He was gaining nothing tearing down the father in the daughter's eyes. "Come on—I'll walk you to your cabin."

She shook her head and rose. Her ebullience had leaked out. She looked like a sleepy little girl.

Ruff took her arm, wrapped it around his own, and took her to her cabin which was on the stern.

At the doorway she said, "I didn't mean to go cold on you."

"My own fault. A lot of bad energy swirling around me tonight. I should have kept my mouth shut."

"We'll try again . . . maybe," she said.

"Maybe."

She turned her cheek toward him and he gave her the peck she seemed to expect, said good-night, and watched the door close.

"Going for the young ones now?" Sally Shore said from the shadows. She still wore her dress, and as Ruff walked to her, he could see that she was shivering.

"She's not that young," Justice answered.

"She seems real experienced," Sally said, and there was coldness in her tone.

"Why, Sally Shore," Justice said, grinning.

"Ah, shut up. You men—all the same."

"You're going to have to tell me about him someday."

"*Him?* Ah, Christ, dry up, Justice." She was still shivering.

As Ruff stepped to her, he put his arms around her. She didn't pull away when he drew her to his chest, holding her closely. For a minute there she felt like a woman—soft, small, sagged against him, her breasts rising and falling as she breathed. Then she suddenly pushed away. There was anger and a fleeting, unspoken question in her eyes. She turned and walked away, her stride like a seaman's again now that she had remembered she was the captain.

Ruff smiled, shook his head, and started toward his own cabin.

They came out of the darkness like warring shadows, thick, overpowering, deadly. The one on

Justice's left was tall and broad. Steel glinted coldly in his hand. The knife blade flashed at Ruff's belly, but Justice was able to step back and kick out savagely. His boot caught wrist bone, and there was an ugly snapping sound as a man cried out in pain.

"Get him," the one on the right growled, but he was going to have to do the getting himself. The shadowy figure stepped right in, truncheon or pipe raised high over head.

Justice moved inside, locking his arms around the man's chest. The truncheon fell harmlessly past his shoulder. Ruff ran the assailant back toward the rail. The man's back hit hard against it and he flailed wildly at Justice with clawing hands. Ruff put his hand under the man's chin and shoved. The thug tried to protest but only a strangled snarl came out. Ruff pushed a little harder, as if he would lift the man's head from his neck. When he stepped back, he continued to push and the attacker went overboard, splashing into the black Missouri, swept away by the current.

Ruff turned back. The man with the broken wrist was a volunteer: he was standing on the rail, and when Justice started that way, he leapt. Ruff watched him fall into the water and vanish.

"Sorry, Sally," Justice said. She would be two short on her crew.

The big man, he had thought, could have been Lydell Cherry, but, no, there was Cherry in the pilothouse talking to Cap MacAdoo. Ruff stood in the darkness taking a few slow deep breaths. Then, there being no point in trying much else, he went off to his cabin, undressed, and went to sleep.

Morning brought Fort Mandan into view around a bend in the big river.

There was no town around Mandan, just a collection of Indian tepees and a few shacks huddled against the wall of the fort for protection. There were trees along the river here, great oaks and sycamores, but back away from the Missouri there was only the endless miles of flat dry plains.

The *Jacksonville* veered toward shore, its toots on the whistle bringing the Indians from their tepees and soldiers to the shore to stand staring.

Ruff was in buckskins, his hat tilted back on his head, his boot propped up on the rail. He saw Nancy Hawkins coming toward him, waving a cheery hand. Her dress was much more casual, much more suitable. A divided buckskin skirt, knee-high boots, white blouse and buckskin jacket, Spanish hat hanging down her back on a thong.

" 'Morning," she said brightly. "We made good time, didn't we? And no troubles at all! You worry too much, Mister Justice."

"It looks like it," he agreed just to save a discussion. He didn't, however, restrain his eyes. He looked her up and down, frankly enjoying the curve and slant of her body. Her breasts forced themselves against the fabric of her blouse with each breath as if eager to be free, unrestrained.

Onshore, nameless faces stared up at them as the steamboat nudged against the rickety gray wood wharf and was tied up among the canoes. Cap MacAdoo tooted the whistle twice more and then shut the steam engines down.

"Come on, Justice," Sally Shore called out from the gangplank. "Going with me?"

"Where?"

"The fort, for Christ's sake. Where else would I go? Quit playing with the girls and come on."

Nancy tittered a little and turned her face away. Ruff touched her shoulder in farewell. He saw Lt. John Lewis Weeks standing in the shade cast by the wheelhouse, glaring at him, and Ruff lifted a hand to him. The young officer ignored it. No manners, Ruff thought. He met the impatient Sally Shore at the gangway.

"What's the hurry, Sally?"

"You'll find out. Let's go. I want to talk to the commanding officer here. I want some cut wood, and I want it now."

"They can't have much—" A distant whistle interrupted Justice. He looked around in puzzlement. Sally Shore grabbed his arm roughly.

"Come on."

"What was that?"

"If you must know . . . well, have your own look." Her pointing finger lifted southward and Ruff saw it then. A tiny white speck floating against the Missouri, growing larger as it plowed toward them, belching steam from its stacks. A paddle-wheeler. A steamboat in their wake.

"Who the hell is that?" he asked.

"Who? Griff Oakland, that's who. Who else would it be?"

"Who the hell's Griff Oakland?"

"Justice, you amaze me. What river do you run, anyway?"

He didn't stop to point out that the river he generally ran was composed of prairie grass, coulees, broken hills, and buffalo. He followed her along toward the fort, glancing back once to see the implacable white paddle-wheeler steaming toward Mandan.

Maj. Hawkins had descended from the steamboat now and he was returning the salutes of the soldiers on the wharf as he and Lt. Weeks walked toward the fort. Hawkins looked slightly perturbed, as if he had expected a brass band.

"You know the commander of this post?" Sally asked.

"Simmons. Yes, I do." And Ruff liked him. Simmons was a lonely man, a good soldier, but essentially a loner who was out of place in army company. No doubt he would retire out of the army, still a major most likely—promotions didn't come easy on the frontier—still a loner.

"I thought he'd come out to greet Hawkins, but maybe he wouldn't know Hawkins was on the boat."

And knowing Simmons, Ruff was certain he wouldn't have cared, but he didn't say anything. They had gone into the post through a side gate and now walked along the crudely constructed split-log plank-walk toward the commander's office.

The first sergeant looked up. "Oh, God, no! Not Ruffin T. Justice." He stood and thrust out a narrow hand. "Don't tell me you've been given to us, Mister Justice."

"No. Your good luck, Hank. I'm with Miss Shore here. She'd like to see Major Simmons."

Sgt. Henry Thomas glanced toward the commander's door as if it were a sanctum he seldom penetrated—in fact, that was what it was. Simmons spent most of his time in his office alone, reading. He didn't like to be summoned unless there was a full-scale Indian attack.

"I'll see." The sergeant went in and, after a few muffled words, returned. "Go on in, Ruff, Miss Shore."

Simmons was closing a leather-bound book eight or ten inches thick when they went in. His office was in darkness but for the desk lamp.

He stood wearily, like an overtired college professor greeting lively and incomprehensible students. "Ruffin. Miss Shore. What can I do for you?"

Sally leapt right in. "I'm making a supply run to Fort Benton. Steamboating. What I need from you, Major Simmons, is cut wood."

"We need cut wood around here as well," Simmons said. He rubbed his eyes. "We have very little, you've probably noticed."

"All the same, I've got to get upriver. Benton is cut off, the way I hear it. I've got supplies and weapons for them."

The door opened again and Ruff could almost see the pain in Simmons' eye. "What is it, Hank?"

"A Major Hawkins, sir. New post commander, Fort Benton. Wants to see you."

Simmons looked at Ruff as if this were all his doing, then he nodded to Hank Thomas. A moment later Hawkins and Weeks swept in. Simmons rose, saluted, shook hands, and offered chairs.

"What about that wood, Major?" Sally demanded. She hadn't grown any less pushy between Lincoln and Mandan.

Simmons looked puzzled again. Maj. Hawkins, who was leaning back in his chair—quite self-satisfied, apparently—put in, "I believe our charming captain does need additional fuel to see us through upriver, sir. If you do have a surplus, it would be greatly appreciated."

"All right, yes," Simmons said, as if he hoped they would all go away if he gave in. "But . . ."

The door opened again and Simmons looked ready to crack as he glowered at his first sergeant. Henry Thomas was apologetic. "Sir, I got another civilian out here."

"Have him wait."

"He says this meeting concerns him. His name's Griff Oakland."

"My God," Sally said, "what did the bastard do, swim ashore?"

He didn't appear to be wet when he burst into the major's office a moment later, but Griff Oakland had been doing some fast moving—his chest rose and fell excitedly, his face was flushed crimson. He could hardly speak at first for lack of breath.

"All lies . . ." he finally gasped. "All damn lies, Major . . . This woman . . ." A finger wavered in front of Sally Shore's hostile eyes. The rest of the sentence got lost in the general clamor as Sally, the major, and Oakland began speaking at once. It took Simmons a while to get order. He looked nearly desperate to clear these intruders away.

"What is this now? Mr. Oakland first."

"She's telling everyone she got the contract to supply Benton. It ain't so."

"I got the army provisions," Sally said, surging forward, her face nearly meeting Oakland's. "I got a contract . . ."

"I got a contract, too. Want to see it?" Oakland flourished a sheaf of papers. "Regimental headquarters give me this option contract. What the hell is this, Sally, trying to keep out the competition? You read paragraph two there—" He held it toward her, but Sally knocked paragraph two to the floor. "It says, 'No field commander can . . . 'Ah, shit, it says that anyone who wants a shot at this contract gets a chance."

"But I've got the goods," Sally said, tapping her breast.

"Yeah, well, I've got 'em too! Paid for out of my own pocket since you tried to shut me out of this without a fair chance," Oakland said.

"The hell I did," Sally shot back. Her tone made it clear that that was exactly what she *had* done.

Simmons wanted order again. "We have two steamboats here? Each trying to get upriver to Benton?"

"Yes, sir."

"I don't have enough cut wood for the both of you."

"I was here first," Sally began.

Simmons waved a silencing hand. "You're welcome to cut what you need. You have axes? Help yourselves."

And that was it as far as Simmons was concerned. After shaking hands with Major Hawkins and saying he hoped he saw him again soon, which he didn't, he settled in behind his desk with his massive book and gratefully sighed as his visitors filed out.

"I'll beat you upriver yet, Sally," Oakland promised her. "You know damn well you kept everyone else from finding out about this until it was too late." Oakland waved a fist. "You'll see. You'll see!" He jammed a hat on his head and stormed out of the building.

"Shame on you," Ruff Justice said.

Sally smiled. "Come on, Ruff, we've got some wood to cut."

"Known this Oakland long?" Justice asked as they went outside.

"Seems like all my life. Years on the river, anyway. He's a snake. If the army awards him the contract, there'll be plenty of short loads coming up the Missouri. He'll skim what he can and cheap-good what he can. That's the truth. He's like that; he'll kill to get what he wants. He has before."

"You've got something particular in mind."

"Not now," she said.

Ruff shrugged. If she didn't want to talk about it, fine. He could see the other steamboat, the twin wheels on its side sitting dead in the water. On deck someone waved a fist at the *Jacksonville.*

"Your crews all know each other?" Ruff asked.

"We all know each other. Bums and wharf rats and crooks is what Oakland hires."

"It doesn't get any easier, does it?" Ruff said quietly.

"What?"

"We had Indians and a rough river. Now we've got Oakland to worry about."

"Ah, hell Justice, you worry too much. Let me see those hands of yours, tall man." When Ruff showed them to her, she nodded with satisfaction. "Yeah, those'll fit an ax handle just fine."

4

The woods rang with the sound of axes falling. Sweat rained from Justice's brow as he swung, cutting deep into the heartwood of the big oak. He stepped back as she started to sway and creak and finally topple. When it hit the ground, members of Sally's crew armed with saws and hatchets moved in to cut it into lengths.

Justice found another dead tree and got to it. The day had cooled, a thin river fog hanging over the Missouri. It did nothing to chill the body. Ruff's hands were blistered, his shoulders sore.

"There's one, Curly," someone behind Justice said. He turned to see Oakland pointing at the tree he had selected.

"There's a man chose it already," Curly replied.

"Get him the hell away from it, then," Oakland ordered. "That's my wood."

"But, Captain—"

"Damn you, Curly. Didn't you hear me?"

Curly looked reluctant to try it. A big, slope-shouldered man with a mat of hair spilling from the V of his shirt front, he was dirty and glossed with sweat. He had a big double-bit ax in his thick hands. A second sailor arrived.

"Curly, what's up?"

Now that there were two of them, Curly thought the captain had had a fine idea. "We're movin' this cowboy out of here and takin' this oak," Curly answered.

"All right." The second sailor didn't have any objections either.

"Take it easy, boys," Ruff said. "A man could get hurt."

"Yeah, a man could get hurt," Curly said. "Get out of our way. We need the wood."

Justice cursed himself for leaving his gun belt on ship. He hadn't planned on shooting any trees down, though. Curly and his little partner pressed ahead. Curly's ax was across his body now, the head slightly elevated. His fingers opened and closed around the curved hickory handle.

"Move it, tall man."

"Can't do it, boys." Ruff's own ax came up. "These things would make a terrible mess of muscle and bone, Curly."

"You'll find out, I guess." Curly sounded confident now, but the other one didn't look so sure about things.

"Curly—"

"Shut up. You heard the captain."

"The hell with the captain."

"You goin' to tell Oakland that?"

"No." The little man shook his head. Just another soldier going reluctantly into battle.

Curly swung his ax. The blow was unexpected, wild. Ruff ducked and the double-bit ax whipped past his head to embed itself in the dead oak. Curly's eyes went wild as he realized that the ax was stuck, that Justice had a weapon of his own.

"Get him," he shouted at his partner, but that one dropped his ax and took to his heels.

"You could have hurt me badly," Ruff Justice said. He placed his ax aside. "I wouldn't care to run around without a head—no place to put my hat."

Curly had backed up, but now, as Ruff put his ax down, he puffed himself up again and came forward.

"I don't need no damn ax to take your head off, tall man. I'll rip it off with my bare hands."

He tried it.

Curly roared and came at Justice with his massive arms outflung trying to wrap Ruff in a bear hug. All that got him was an uppercut to the point of his chin, which sent him staggering back a step.

He tried science. Curly circled left, flicking out his left hand like a bear's paw. Ruff watched it, timed it, stepped to his own left away from the punch, and stuck a sharp jab into Curly's face. Curly's lips split and he shook his head dully. Ruff hit him again and the big man roared again with anger.

Ruff ducked a looping right and stuck his left into Curly's face again. Curly's nostrils began to leak blood. When he came toward Justice again, his knees were wobbling. Justice hooked a hard right over the top. It landed flush on Curly's ear and Curly went down and stayed down.

"It beats an ax in the skull," Ruff told him.

Curly didn't hear it; he was asleep.

Ruff yanked the big sailor's ax from the oak, placed it on the ground, the head on a rock, and stamped on it, snapping the handle off. Then, looking at his blistered hands and shaking his head, he got to work felling the tree.

It was late afternoon before Sally had all the wood she could carry, and the *Jacksonville* sat puffing and groaning, straining at the tethers of its lines like a horse eager to be off, the full head of steam in the twin boilers occasionally filling the air with the whine of the relief valves.

Oakland was ready to leave as well. He waved his arms at the last sailors, rushing toward the boat with armloads of wood. If they had been any slower, Justice thought Oakland would have left them behind because Sally Shore had ordered the lines thrown off and the *Jacksonville* was turning into the current, her stacks spewing white smoke, her big stern wheel turning, throwing up loops of silver water.

The whistle on Oakland's boat sounded three times and her lines too were frantically thrown off. Ruff stood on the upper deck and watched, shaking his head. He smiled, but it was a little grim. Someone was going to get killed. It would be a wonder if a lot of people didn't get it.

Oakland's boat was named the *River Nymph* and she was well-cared-for apparently; she was freshly painted, as was the *Jacksonville*, and her engines sounded clean and smooth.

"What's all this about?" Nancy Hawkins asked.

Ruff turned to smile at her. "Money. They figure to rule the upper river for a good many years to come, maybe supply all four posts above Lincoln. The army's needful of all sorts of supplies."

"Yes, I'm an army brat. I realize that. Father's not very happy about the turn of events."

"Oh? Why's that?"

"He feels Sally Shore's taken advantage of him. She claimed to have the contract when in fact she didn't. She tried to sneak in ahead of the other bidder. She took Father and me upriver on her boat, wining and dining us."

Justice nodded. He could see how it looked. Whether Sally was guilty of all that scheming or not was irrelevant. One thing was sure: she was a long way from having things locked up now—it was a hazardous way they traveled, the competition smack on their heels.

"Well, Colonel MacEnroe sent me with Sally," Ruff said. "And I suppose that means I'm on her side. Besides, if it's a choice between her and Griff Oakland, Sally wins every time in my book."

"I know what you mean. If Father ever saw the way Oakland was looking at me when we were on shore . . ."

"Worse than the way I look?" Ruff asked, lifting an eyebrow.

"Oh, you. It's just healthy with you, kind of exciting, you know. With Oakland it's like he'd like to peel me."

"We'll see he doesn't get the chance."

They heard three shots from the shore and they moved to the starboard rail along with half the crew. They saw him then, moving toward the river's edge, firing at something they couldn't see beyond the trees.

"They've got him cornered," someone said.

"Sioux," said Lt. Weeks.

Ruff couldn't see any Indians, but he saw the young man look their way, sprint for the water, and dive in. His gun was left behind as he swam toward the *Jacksonville*. He was tall, young, and wore jeans and a white shirt.

Cap MacAdoo had put the wheel over and they were approaching shore now as the swimmer neared them. There was a jerk when the paddle wheel slowed and then stopped as they picked up the swimmer. The *River Nymph* steamed on past, hooting its whistle derisively.

Sally Shore was fuming, but there hadn't been much of a choice. The swimmer appeared to be in difficulty. They couldn't have just left him, although Oakland apparently would have.

"Give him a line, boys," Sally said. She made a circular motion with her hand toward the wheelhouse and Cap tugged on the throttle, bringing the stern wheel to life again.

Ruff wandered forward and he was there when the young man came up over the low bow of the *Jacksonville*.

He stood, trembling slightly with exhaustion. He looked shoreward and then back to his rescuers.

"Thanks," he said, "they nearly had me."

"Sioux?" Weeks asked excitedly.

"Yes. Spotted Sioux. I was trapping on their river and they took exception."

"We didn't hear any guns but yours."

"No. Bows and arrows was what they had. Young bucks."

"They've got a gun now," Ruff Justice said, and the man's quick yellow-green eyes met his.

"What?"

"They've got your gun, haven't they?"

The kid grinned and scratched his head. "Well, I guess they have, yes." He added, "And everything else I owned, including a load of prime pelts. My name's Wyatt, Farley Wyatt." He stuck out a hand to the nearest man, who happened to be Weeks, and then was introduced around. His eyes narrowed when he heard Justice's name.

"So you're the one, are you? Thought you'd be older."

"I feel older."

Sally Shore broke up the party. "You men get back to work. Let's go! Look at Oakland, damn him, around the bend already." She went off swearing to herself. Maj. Hawkins, who didn't think much of Justice's company, took Nancy away, and Weeks trailed subserviently along.

"Come on," Justice said. "I might have some dry clothes to fit you."

"Never seen a steamboat up this far. I see Jack Troll and his rats now and then. At a distance and from behind my sights, but never a steamer. Did I cause someone trouble? The woman in the sailor suit didn't look happy."

Ruff explained it as briefly as possible. Wyatt looked apologetic and said he was. Ruff took him at his word for now. It bothered him, however, that he had seen no Sioux. And that he had never heard of Spotted Sioux drifting this far east.

Farley Wyatt, when he was dried out and dressed in Ruff's black jeans and cotton shirt, proved to be a tall, narrow, wiry man of twenty-five with the scars of wilderness living on his torso and arms. He had reddish hair, which waved in front when he dried and combed it, a schoolboy's smile, and eyes that knew more than they were telling. He impressed Ruff as a man you'd like to have on your side in a fight, but not one to sit down to a poker table with.

"I wonder if the lady can use another hand," Wyatt said, buttoning his shirt.

"Probably. We lost two overboard the other night. Are you a sailing man?"

"I've worked on the flatboats downriver. Same thing, I guess. I've got to do something—when I lost those furs I lost my wintering-up money. I don't care to end up hungry at Christmas, buried for New Year's."

"That's a long way off."

"So's home. I need work."

When Wyatt had gone, looking for Sally Shore, Ruff sat pondering the water spots left behind on his floor. He could make nothing of his suspicions, and so he went up on deck again. At least Wyatt was willing to work. Ruff felt that, so far, he had just been a passenger on the boat, contributing very little.

Looking forward, he could see the *River Nymph*, nearer now. The *Jacksonville* definitely seemed to be the faster boat. Sally had that throttle open, fighting time and the river current, which, Ruff noted, was growing quicker now. Snags and sandbars had begun to dot the river, ripples marking their locations. There would be no traveling in the dark tonight—and the sun was already going down.

In another ten minutes the two steamboats were side by side. Men shouted remarks that couldn't be heard above the slap of the wheels, the pulsing of the engines. Once an object was thrown from the *River Nymph*, but it fell harmlessly into the water.

They pulled even and then passed the *River Nymph*, racing on into the darkness, which was approaching rapidly now. The trees on the western bank cast shadows on the water. The sun dropped behind the big oaks, orange and huge.

"We're going to have to anchor soon, Sally," Ruff heard Cap yell from the wheelhouse.

"Keep going."

"Can't see the bars, Sally."

"Damn you, Cap. You must be getting old."

"I lost one boat this way, Sally. I'd hate to have it happen again."

"Another mile." She stood at the rail, peering upriver intently, willing her boat on. "Just another mile, Cap."

Looking back, Ruff saw that the *River Nymph* was already out of sight. Maybe Oakland had already anchored down.

Fifteen minutes later the big paddle wheel slowed and then stopped.

Nancy Hawkins, looking fresh and bright in a divided green skirt and white blouse, found Justice. "I thought steamboats tied up along the shore. I didn't think they anchored in the middle of the river," she said.

"With Indians onshore they do," Ruff answered.

"Are we in Indian territory now?" she asked, her amber eyes getting just a little wide.

"Yes. They're out there now, watching."

"But they surely won't bother us."

"Why not?"

"Well, it just doesn't seem there's any point in it," Nancy said hopefully.

Ruff didn't encourage her fantasy. "There's every point in it. We've got plenty of goods on board. A fortune, in fact, to an Indian. Think of it—what wagon train ever carried weapons and ammunition, food, blankets, pots and pans, knives and axes like we've got back there?"

"But they wouldn't dare . . ."

"Sure they'd dare. The exception would be an

Indian who wouldn't dare, who would sacrifice his pride in manhood to caution. And they don't need their war ponies to try it either. The Sioux fought long before he had horses."

"If they came, well, they'd want . . ."

He knew what she meant. "Yes, they'd want you first. We're not carrying anything worth more than a white woman to the Indians."

Nancy shivered a little—maybe she was able to convince herself it was because of the slowly increasing night chill. Ruff looped his arm around her and squeezed her briefly.

Sally found them standing like that. She made a clicking sound with her tongue, and Ruff slowly turned his head toward her. She looked manly standing in her captain's cap and coat before the last glow of sunset. The tilt and thrust of her body was masculine. Sometimes she almost fooled Ruff Justice, but not often. There was a woman down deep under all that. He could see it, smell it, sense it.

Just now the woman was a little testy. "You got to be doing that all the time, Justice? Good God, from the moment I first laid eyes on you you've been touching and squeezing and poking at the girls."

Nancy cleared her throat rather dramatically and pushed away from Ruff, offering him a slight, amused smile before she said good-night to both of them and hurried away.

"You're a help," Justice said.

"Yeah, well, you need some help. What do you think's going to happen when that sauced-up major catches you with his baby girl?"

"Sauced-up?"

"Yeah, he's in his cabin looking at the bottom of a bottle of sour mash. It wasn't long ago that the bottle was full; I know, it came out of my stores."

Ruff shook his head. It didn't surprise him. There was usually a reason for an officer getting an assignment out here on the fringe of the known world—

and it wasn't usually a reward for meritorious service. There were good officers and men on the frontier, but there were also a lot of losers, semicriminals, misfits, loners, drinkers. Ruff had been wondering vaguely which category Maj. Hawkins fell into.

"I want you to take a party ashore, Ruff."

"Now?"

"Yes. I want to take on all the wood we can whenever we can—so long as it doesn't cost us river time—and that means when we're moored."

"It's not the best thing in the world to chop wood at night, Sally."

"I know. Do what you can. We'll have to rely on what dead wood we can collect, I suppose. I gave Cherry a dinghy. I don't know how much wood she'll carry, use your own discretion." She looked at Ruff in a way that undervalued that discretion.

"Me and Cherry."

"Yeah. Taffy and Joe Heck will go along. I know you and Cherry had some kind of squabble, but he told me he's not carrying a grudge."

"That's kind of Cherry," Ruff said dryly.

"You just ooze sarcasm, don't you? By the way, where's that friend of yours?"

"What friend?"

"This Farley Wyatt. I hired him on and haven't seen him since. I wanted to send him ashore instead of Taffy."

"I haven't seen Wyatt. What makes him my friend?"

"You gave him your pants, didn't you?" Sally asked. Her logic was hardly impeccable, but it was interesting.

Ruff found Cherry at the port rail; the first mate had a painter in hand, holding the dinghy to while two other nervous sailors waited.

"Where you been? What's the gun for?" He nodded at Justice's .56 Spencer repeater.

"I didn't hurry because of the moon. Wait for it to rise and we'll be able to half see what we're doing. As for the gun . . . you ought to be able to figure that out, Cherry."

The small man in the white shirt was called Taffy. He sat looking to the dark woods. "They're out there, aren't they?"

"They're out there."

They waited another five minutes while Taffy and Joe Heck ran back to their quarters for their own weapons. Cherry was already wearing a belt gun. He and Justice sat staring at each other across the length of the rowboat until the two others returned. Then, with the rim of the moon peering over the ranks of trees along the eastern shore, they pushed away from the *Jacksonville* and dipped their oars, moving silently across the dark and silky water toward shore.

5

It was still and dark. The moon cast a net of moving shadows beneath the outstretched branches of the river trees. The boat nudged against the shore and they leapt silently from it, dragging it into the shadows. There they crouched for a time, moon-bright eyes searching, their ears listening intently until they could hear only the singing of blood in their own ears, the distant croaking of frogs in the cattails along an oxbow.

Ruff Justice liked none of this. But he had hired on. He was going to do the job.

Along the river between Fort Mandan and Fort Union, as they were, he didn't expect to find a large body of hostiles, but experience had shown him it was the renegades, the young bucks, the reservation-embittered ones roaming the country that were to be feared. Red Cloud, encircling Fort Benton, poised to make a dash for Canada if necessary, wasn't going to send out small foraying parties. It was pointless. The young bucks, on the other hand—those who had grown up without the chance to fight the wars of their fathers, to sit and tell their tales around the campfire and strut their bonnets in front of the women—were the ones who came looking for coup . . . at almost any cost.

"Scrounge around," Cherry told the others. "See

what you can find loose, then let's get the hell out of here."

Cherry and Ruff Justice had finally found common ground. Ruff sat back on his heels, his rifle cradled in his arms. Cherry didn't like it at first—he was working and Ruff wasn't—but before he had opened his mouth to complain, he realized that it wasn't such a bad idea to have a man with a rifle watching over you while you stooped and scraped for wood.

The first load was taken on quickly and they rowed back to the *Jacksonville* feeling a little relieved. Taffy's shirt was soaked through with sweat, and the night was cool. Ruff gave him an encouraging glance that didn't do much to chase away the cold fear gnawing at the sailor.

They off-loaded the wood and returned to the shore. They had to spread out now and work deeper into the woods to find much. Ruff worked with one hand and kept his grip on the Spencer with the other. He had just placed a three-foot length of oak in the rowboat when he saw the other boat.

It was drifting toward shore, silent and dark. The moon was like a beacon behind it, but all it did was silhouette the men in the boat, leaving them faceless.

"Hey, Justice, I—" Cherry began one of his endless complaints.

"Quiet. Get down too."

"What the hell's the matter?" Then he too saw the boat making its way toward them.

"Who is it?" Ruff whispered.

"Has to be Oakland, don't it?"

"Yes." Ruff nodded. It almost had to be Griff Oakland's crew coming ashore to gather wood for the *River Nymph*'s fireboxes. The boat touched shore several hundred yards downriver. Justice could see no more of them then.

"Let's get on back," Ruff said.

"We've only got half a load."

"I don't think we're up to a night fight, do you?"

"Dammit, the lady wants wood! I follow orders."

"Cherry . . ." He put a hand on Lydell Cherry's shoulder, but the big man pulled away—he had his orders. Now from downriver Ruff could hear the sound of a saw and a pair of axes and he grumbled an indistinct curse.

Good thinking. Make plenty of noise. Wake the Sioux from here to Montana.

Ruff couldn't pull out alone and so he got back to work, but there was considerable distaste for the project building in his mind. He looked around, not seeing Cherry or Taffy anywhere. Joe Heck, who had, quite understandably, decided to try sticking close to the boat, was just visible in the web of shadows to the north along the shore.

The axes to the south had ceased their ringing.

Ruff didn't like that either, but he wasn't sure what it meant. He was sure what the next sound meant: agony. A man screamed in pain and terror. Justice sprinted toward the cry, his hat flying free, his right hand cocking the Spencer, throwing a big .56 cartridge into the breech.

The man loomed up before Ruff, a shadow sprung to life. Justice never found out who it was. He saw the gun in the man's hand and he fired from the hip. He never slowed his pace. The Spencer ripped into the man's body, shattering his spine, pulping vital organs as the lead slug expanded. The man's mouth was open in a silent scream, black blood leaking from his chest as Ruff Justice leapt over the body and continued on through the confusing tangle of living trees and their shadowy images. The moon flitted overhead above the black limbs of the big oaks.

Ruff stopped, panting, listening. Where? The night was suddenly silent, and it shouldn't have been. The echo of the gunshot still rang in his ears. He could hear the crickets distantly. Nothing else. Someone moved in the underbrush and Ruff slowly swung the big muzzle of his Spencer that way.

It was Taffy. The little sailor stepped forward, his face dead white in the pale moonlight, his eyes black smudges. He saw Ruff.

"I think . . ." Taffy said. Then he fell forward on his face.

Ruff scooted to him, but it was too late. Taffy was still breathing, but in another minute he wouldn't be. There was an arrow in his neck from side to side. The sailor's lips moved a little. His blood-coated tongue flickered out. He died before it had pulled back into the dark recess of his mouth.

There was a whisper of sound to Ruff's left. The Indian came out of the brush, war ax raised high, and Justice, using the Spencer like a club, laid the stock of the rifle across the Sioux's throat. He went down strangling on blood, gasping for breath through a crushed trachea.

There was more movement to Ruff's right and he switched the rifle, aiming it that way. Lydell Cherry came out of the trees, his shirt torn, his face smeared with dirt or blood, or both.

"It's me!" Cherry hissed. He stared at the Indian on the ground, still writhing, strangling. Ruff finished the Sioux with his bowie as Cherry watched, stunned.

"I lost my gun," Cherry said.

"Where's Heck?" Ruff asked, giving Cherry his Colt.

"I haven't seen him."

"Taffy's dead."

"I know . . ." Shots from the river interrupted their hurried conversation. They looked at each other and started running toward the boat.

Before they got to the shore, they found Heck. His scalp was missing and his throat had been cut. His caution hadn't been enough to save him.

"Goddammit all," Cherry said.

Ruff put his rifle in the boat and shouted, "Come on, let's do something about it."

The Indians were attacking the riverboats. There were many logs around the *Jacksonville*, enough to indicate to Ruff that the Sioux had drifted to the steamboat lying on those logs; then, when they were ready, they had tried to take it.

There was gunfire on board the *Jacksonville* now, a small fire near the texas deck. Ruff shipped his oars long enough to pick a boarding Sioux off a line near the front of the steamboat. He fell screaming into the water as the .56 spoke its death chant.

Cherry missed a shot with the handgun—it was out of range for the Colt—but Ruff scored again. The moon was behind the Sioux and they seemed to be targets in a shooting gallery. Justice picked one off a log as he rose up and reached for the taffrail. The fire on the texas deck had gone out and now Ruff could see that the Sioux had been beaten back.

Two braves leapt for the water from the bow. One of them made it alive. The other folded up as Justice shot him and he was sacrificed to the river gods.

Then it was still again, so silent that it ate at the nerves. There had to be more Indians around—on the boat, in the water, on the logs—but there weren't. They had gone, carried away like smoke on the wind.

"Hail her," Ruff said to Cherry.

"Why?"

"Hail the boat—I don't want them taking us for Indians." Or for Oakland's men. What had happened to the *River Nymph*'s wood party?

Cherry glowered at Ruff over the pile of wood between them. He hailed the boat. After a moment, an answer came—a voice Ruff couldn't identify—and they rowed in silence toward the *Jacksonville*.

The mood on board was quiet, determined, and a little shocked. Sally walked the decks silently, shaking her head. A cabin door had been half battered down. Another sailor lay dead, his blood pooled darkly under him, spreading slowly across the oak planking. Sally met Justice and Cherry as they climbed aboard the *Jacksonville*.

"Howdy, Ruff," was all she said.

"Everything okay?"

She shrugged—how could everything be okay? All Justice had meant was, Is the *Jacksonville* still intact and can you carry on? The lady had a will of iron, but this was enough to shake even Sally . . . temporarily.

Within minutes she was herself again. Shouting orders, scolding her watch for being taken in by the floating logs. "*That* better not happen again. You start shooting at driftwood if necessary. You hear me?" She pushed her fingers into her hair in irritation—not at the sailors, but at fate, herself.

The cargo had been molested, but not much was missing. A rifle or two from one of the crates, a few hats. "What the well-dressed Sioux needs," Justice muttered.

"What?"

"Nothing." Ruff's own hat was back onshore somewhere—a thirty-dollar stetson—but he didn't feel like going back to look for it.

"We didn't lose much anyway."

"Except people," Ruff said a little harshly.

"I know it, Justice." Sally became a human being, a woman, for fifteen seconds. Her hand touched Ruff's arm. "But we both know we can't do anything about it. Maybe it's my fault they're dead—I gave them a job when they were hungry. Maybe it's their daddy's fault for wanting to lay with momma one cold night. I'm not worrying about them—you wouldn't think much of me if I did." She went back to being captain of a steamboat again.

Ruff saw Maj. Hawkins staggering toward them, weaving and stumbling, a Schofield pistol dangling from his hand. He didn't see Ruff Justice as he walked past.

"Bottle fatigue," Sally quipped.

The engineer had grease on his white shirt, smudges on his hard, lined face. He found Sally as she toured the decks, and he reported. "Cap'n, the number-one engine's down."

"Down! What do you mean down?"

"Down. Somebody took a sledge and cracked the main bearing."

"And what?" Sally reached boiling point faster than her steam engines. "What in the hell are you talking about, Ed?"

"During the attack. We grabbed up our guns and got to fighting. When we went back below, number one was down. Cracked bearing."

"You can fix it."

"Sure I can fix it," Ed said, wiping his forehead with a greasy forearm. "Ten hours."

"Ten hours! To replace a bearing?"

"And the casing. That'll have to be handmade. We got no parts. You don't figure on this sort of thing. Time we pull the drive piston and fit a new bearing—ten hours is an optimistic estimate, Sally."

Ruff stood there listening. By now Sally Shore must have been wondering the same thing he was: *who*?

Who had taken the sledgehammer and tried to destroy the *Jacksonville*'s engines?

It wasn't the Indians, that was for sure. Someone on board the boat had used the attack to his own advantage, slipping into the *Jacksonville*'s engine room to try to disable her. And it had worked.

"Oakland is the only one to profit from this," Sally said as if continuing the thought in Ruff's mind.

"He couldn't have gotten anyone on board during the fight, Sally."

"No."

They looked at each other, understanding what

was indicated—someone on board the *Jacksonville* was an Oakland man, intent on wrecking Sally's performance in front of the major, intent on wrecking the *Jacksonville.*

But who? Sally was quick to stick up for her crew. "I've had these men with me through hell and high water, Justice. I'd bet most anything on the lot of them."

"Even Cherry?"

"Especially Cherry. Besides, he was with *you*, wasn't he, Ruff?"

"He was with me. Do we *know* this was done during the attack, though? It could have happened anytime since we've been moored."

"Maybe. What do you think, Ed?"

The engineer, who had a huge wrench in his hands and grease on his powerful forearms, turned toward them thoughtfully. "It could be. I don't think so, but it's possible. Anyone could just duck in and wreak havoc. Maybe the attack interrupted *his* work."

"It could have happened anytime?"

"Since we shut down," Ed replied. "Yes, it could have happened earlier. We wouldn't have noticed until we completed lubrication."

That was that, then—they knew nothing and had a ship full of suspects. "Do your best, Ed," was the last thing Sally said as they went back on deck.

They were cleaning up the remains of the fire damage on the texas deck. Elsewhere things were silent. Guards with rifles circled the wheelhouse, watching for more Indians.

"Will the Sioux be back, Ruff?" Sally asked.

"No telling. Like I told you, it's a mighty tempting target. They'll be wary, but I wouldn't be surprised if they have themselves another try."

They climbed to the upper deck and started toward the wheelhouse. They passed Farley Wyatt and Sally turned on him.

"Where the hell have you been, Wyatt?"

"Nowhere special. Trying to help out." The kid shrugged. He had a nice grin and he flashed it now.

Sally didn't respond. "I was looking all over for you a while back. I couldn't find you."

"Sorry, Captain."

"Yes. You report to Lydell Cherry and have him put you where he wants you."

"Sure, Captain." Wyatt smiled again with the same result. No result.

Ruff said, "I notice you found yourself a belt gun, Wyatt."

The kid touched his holster as if surprised to find it there. It was an army regulation-issue Schofield revolver. "Yeah—they had a bunch of them back there and I figured I might need one."

"Stay out of those supplies," Sally said sternly.

"Sure, Captain. I just didn't want to go around unarmed. I couldn't find anyone to ask when the Sioux hit." He told Ruff, "I left your clothes in your cabin. Thanks." And then he was gone, swaggering away, whistling as he went down the rails to the lower deck by sliding on them.

"Who sent him?" Sally said. "Oakland?"

"You don't trust him?"

"There's something funny about him, isn't there?" Sally asked. "Cocky little son of a bitch, too."

"There's something," Ruff agreed. He recalled the Sioux no one had seen pursuing Farley Wyatt. But there was nothing to do about it. You don't pick a man up out of the river and then throw him back.

"Come on." Sally pushed through into the lighted wheelhouse, where Cap MacAdoo, his face wreathed in pipe smoke and white whiskers, sat reading the *Police Gazette*.

"Howdy," Cap said, amiable despite the concern behind his twinkling blue eyes.

Sally was unrolling her charts, spreading them out on the table, weighting down the recalcitrant corners with little chunks of lead that reminded Ruff very sharply of the weight inside the sap someone had used to try breaking his skull open for him.

"What is it?" he asked, and she showed him.

"There's a fork here. A mile or so on. Move that lantern closer."

"Yes, that's through Hollister Canyon."

"How deep is it?"

"Not deep enough for you."

"I only draw five feet, Justice!"

"It's not deep enough, Sally."

She looked at him challengingly, as if by staring at him long enough and hard enough she could make Ruff give her the answer she wanted.

"It would cut off something like fifty miles, wouldn't it?" Sally asked. "Look at the way the other fork meanders toward Berthold. Dammit! I could leave Oakland behind. He draws too much more water to risk it."

Ruff still couldn't give her the answer she wanted. That stretch of water he remembered only distantly, but when he'd seen it, it had been shallow, silted-up, clotted with rushes. Time had probably left the river fork much the same.

He told her what he thought again, but Sally was tapping her finger on the chart, hardly listening. "Cap, what do you think?"

"I think Justice knows the river better than we do. I think if we run the west fork we're asking for trouble. We can outdistance Oakland by staying on the main channel, Sally. Why ask for trouble?"

"We can outdistance Oakland with a fair start—Ed says ten hours on the bearing." She glanced at her pocket watch. "It'll be dawn. Oakland will be gone by then."

"We'll catch him."

"Cap, sorry to say this, but I think losing the *Birmingham* has made you shy. The time was when you'd take a risk at the drop of a hat."

"Sally, you got everything riding on it. If you rip the bottom out of the *Jacksonville*, you're through."

"There's a chance we'll do that in the main channel, according to Justice!" She shook her head. "I won't lose. I just won't."

"I hope not," Ruff Justice answered. He didn't point out what would happen if she wrecked the *Jacksonville* out here, but he considered it, and he decided he might get back with half of the people to Fort Lincoln if they had to trek across the Sioux-infested plains. Then again he might not. He hoped Sally Shore didn't lose this gamble. If she did, a lot of people were going to lose more than a riverboat.

6

Dawn was graying the eastern skies and Sally Shore was pacing the decks of the *Jacksonville* like a caged big cat. The *River Nymph* was gone, steaming upriver with the first paling of the sky. She had tooted her whistle and steamed by, and Ruff had had to restrain Sally from aiming a pistol shot at her.

"Damn all! Get Ed, Tell him—"

Cap MacAdoo said, "You only slow things up by going by every ten minutes telling him to hurry."

"What's the damn problem?" she asked the skies, although she knew well enough what sorts of problems would be involved in trying to hand-machine precision parts by lantern light in the engine room of a steamboat moored in the middle of the Upper Missouri.

Ruff was getting itchy. There was nothing at all he could do to hurry things up. The engineer was doing the best he could. Sally's ranting wasn't helping much. Justice walked back to the texas deck to have something to do. Farley Wyatt was just slipping out of Nancy Hawkins' cabin.

Justice saw him and at the same moment Wyatt saw Justice. He grinned and waved a hand, walking on without a word of explanation. Ruff went to Nancy's door, tapped on it, and toed it open. She was out; the room was empty.

So what was Wyatt doing there?

Outside the cabin he met Maj. Hawkins traveling under a full head of steam. His face was red, his eyes blurred with alcohol. His breath ran about eighty proof.

"What's holding everything up?" the major demanded.

"Engine's broke down, they're patching it together."

"Broken down!" The major seemed to take it personal. "Why wasn't I told?"

"No idea, sir," Ruff said. Possibly because the major hadn't been in shape to hear anything that was said to him.

"Where's that female captain? Hell of an idea having a woman captain a steamboat."

Ruff nodded. There wasn't much point in saying anything to the major. The man was talking to himself, liking to flail out with his authority. Justice knew he wouldn't care to be a soldier in this man's army.

"That other boat is gone."

"Yes, sir."

"Seems to me it's better-run than this one."

"Could be. It wasn't a breakdown, actually, sir. Someone sabotaged the engine. Probably someone aboard."

"How was that allowed to happen?" Hawkins demanded. Ruff Justice said that he didn't know. The major spent a minute or two looking at his watch. Ruff didn't know if he was computing the steamboat's schedule or figuring if it was time for another shot of whiskey. If he drank the stuff in such piddling amounts as a shot.

There was a belch within the bowels of the *Jacksonville* and a puff of steam discharged from her stacks. Then they heard the surge and gradual smoothing of her engines.

"About time," the major announced to no one. Then he went off toward his cabin.

Ruff returned forward to find Sally. "You intent on taking that west fork?"

"You know I am," Sally said. "I'm going to catch Oakland, pass him, put so much distance between us that there won't be any doubt at all as to which is the faster boat. I'm getting that contract."

"If you don't lose the *Jacksonville*."

"It can't be that bad. I know for a fact that Hardy Keller came down that fork in his flatboat."

"You know how much water a flatboat draws, Sally. Almost none," Justice pointed out.

"Don't you worry, Justice. Let me do the worrying. Just keep your eyes peeled. I can't see the channel for the trees. Is that it over there?"

"Just an oxbow, I think," Justice said. "The fork's on a way."

"Look at that current! It's running good now. That means rain upstream and deep water in the channels."

Ruff nodded in silent agreement. Sally was as remote from his opinions and observations as the major had been. Her mind was made up. Everything else was irrelevant.

They rounded a bend and saw the *River Nymph*, far ahead. Sally let out a slow, healthy oath. The mouth of the west fork opened before them.

"There it is," Ruff Justice said. "If you're determined."

There wasn't much to see. The west fork came in through the oaks like the oxbows they had been seeing all morning. It looked no wider, no deeper.

"You're sure?" Sally asked.

He considered lying to her at that point, but he couldn't bring himself to do it. "I'm sure. That's the west fork."

"Cap!" Sally turned, cupping her hand to her mouth. She pointed out the channel, and Cap, shaking his head worriedly, put the *Jacksonville* into the mouth of the west fork. "I'll show that bastard Oakland," Sally said. She was talking to herself again. "I'll show them all."

It looked like she would. Sally must have been

right about the rain upriver because they steamed ahead smoothly through a wide arm of the big Missouri. The air was fresh and cool, the sky clear, although far to the north clouds were beginning to bunch.

The banks of the river began to rise and soon were actual bluffs as they sailed into Hollister Canyon. By late afternoon they were in the shadow of the western bluffs and they were in trouble.

"Dammit all to hell," Sally said. "Which way, Justice?"

Justice shook his head. Sally had shortcutted them into the damnedest puzzle he had seen for some time. Where normally there was one channel, there were a dozen. The upcountry rain had sent the river branching out in all directions, and the new branches circled low-standing islands, clumps of oak trees miles long, ran into box canyons, and carved frustrating oxbows. To top it all, reeds and cattails had grown up with a rush. They were ten to twelve feet high and they obscured vision in all directions. Sally looked again to Ruff Justice. "Well?"

"Pick your own," Justice said to her.

"You don't know!"

"No. I've been up this way, but I've never seen it like this. Use common sense, I guess—go back."

"Go back, hell!"

"You've got a lot of miles to overtake the *Nymph.*"

"I won't give it up, Justice. One of these channels is the right one."

"Yeah. Which?" Ruff narrowed one eye.

Sally jabbed her finger at a channel that wound around an oak-shaded island. "That one."

Cap opened the throttles and the *Jacksonville* started on, her big paddle wheel slowly turning as they eased into the narrow channel. The oaks reached out and brushed the sides of the boat. The reeds were heavy and Cap had to do some fancywork to keep them from fouling the paddle wheel.

It would be dark before too many hours had passed, and Sally was getting worried. She wasn't alone.

They steamed on through the reed-clotted channel, and when Ruff glanced at Sally, he could see deep concern etched there—the first time that it had showed. Her lips were compressed, tiny lines etched around them, her eyes hard and sharp, trying to penetrate the shadows, the trees, the islands themselves.

The *Jacksonville* hit bottom, hard.

"Dammit!" Sally shouted out as the boat bottomed out. Ruff was thrown against the rail as the *Jacksonville* slowed with an awesome creak and sway and deep, unhealthy groan.

"Reverse it, damn it all, Cap. Reverse it!"

Cap grabbed frantically for the throttle and controls. The engines were slowed, stopped, and then reversed. When the paddle wheel had stopped, it was engaged once more, Cap easing the throttle in, then opening it wide, trying desperately to back the boat off the bar.

It sat there shuddering, the wheel spinning frantically for long minutes. Ruff stood looking at Sally, who was frozen into immobility with frustration and worry. Her body was tensed, fists bunched as if her bodily energy could nudge the *Jacksonville* off the bar.

Then suddenly, the *Jacksonville* came free. She slid from the bar, rolling from side to side momentarily before she settled and sat there like a big placid dog awaiting her master's order.

At the bow Cherry used a long pole to measure the depth of the water from one side to the other. He turned and lifted defeated hands toward Sally Shore.

"You couldn't float a duck here, Sally."

"Get the dinghy out, Cherry. Maybe it's a short bar. We can winch across it if it is."

Ruff heard the boots against the decking and he

turned to see Maj. Hawkins coming on the run. He was fuming.

"What is this? What kind of imcompetence is this?"

In an undertone Ruff told Sally, "Must have knocked him from his bunk."

Sally didn't smile. She was watching as Cherry rowed ahead to check the depth of the water. That pole he was using never went down far.

"I asked you a question, Captain Shore!" Hawkins said too loudly. "What is this?"

"If you're such a damned fool you can't see what it is, I'll explain it to you. The boat ran aground." Then Sally got back to watching Cherry's exercise in frustration. It was no good. They were going to have to back all the way out of the channel and try again to find the proper way.

"Maybe I can find the channel," Ruff said.

"When no one else can," Maj. Hawkins put in.

Ruff ignored him. "If I can get to the high bluffs there and climb them, I could see for a good long way."

"You wouldn't make it before dark," Sally objected.

"Maybe so, maybe no. You're going to have to shut down after dark anyway. Going on like this is a waste of time. Have Cherry get me as near as he can in that rowboat and I'll try it."

"Hell of a climb, Ruff." Sally looked to the high-rising reddish bluffs.

"I said I'll try it."

"Want someone to go along?"

It was Farley Wyatt. The kid was grinning again. Always grinning—and always in the wrong place at the wrong time. Ruff didn't figure he knew Farley well enough.

"No, thanks. I'll go it alone."

"If you're going, better get moving," Sally said.

Cherry had started back toward the steamboat and looked up curiously from the dinghy at Sally's arm signals.

She called down to him. "Hold it there, Cherry. Justice'll tell you what he needs."

"What's that?" Cherry called back.

Sally just waved a hand at him. When she looked at Justice, he was checking the loads in his .44 revolver.

"You don't think they're—"

"I know they're out there," Ruff answered.

"I didn't think of that."

"You *think* of it. Don't forget the Sioux for a minute when you're in their country. They haven't forgotten us, that's for sure." Ruff turned and went past the major and Lt. Weeks, who was standing around looking as ineffectual as always. Nancy was there as well.

"Good luck," she said.

"Thank you." He winked and went on. Climbing over the rail forward, he stopped into the dinghy.

"What's going on?" Cherry demanded.

"I'm going to climb the bluff, try to find the way out of here."

"Climb that?" Cherry's chin lifted toward the steep, crumbling bluff. "Before dark?"

"I'm going to try, yes."

"Never make it."

"All right. Thanks for the encouragement. Start rowing."

Cherry grunted something, then dipped his oars and they moved away from the steamboat into the dark and winding channel. In minutes they could see nothing but the stacks of the *Jacksonville*. The reeds and cattails closed around them like dark-green curtains shutting out the world. Cherry rowed silently, gloomily. Since he had lost his hat, Ruff knotted a red scarf over his head, pirate-fashion, to keep the hair out of his eyes when he climbed. Looking at him, Cherry thought the man looked enough like a buccaneer to bring remembrances of salt water and sailing ships back vividly.

Cherry still didn't like Justice, but he was changing

his opinion of him. The man had nerve, and nerve to spare. If it came to a showdown, he would use caution dealing with Ruff Justice.

"Left up that little branch," Ruff said, guiding Cherry, who had his back to the bow.

Cherry grunted again, looked across his shoulder as he directed the boat.

The bluff loomed overhead now, taller than Justice had thought. It was a good climb, and the settling darkness wouldn't help.

"That's a hundred feet, easy. Look at that sandstone, ready to crumble in your hands," Lydell Cherry said.

"You're a right cheerful man," Ruff said. "No wonder Sally keeps you around."

"What am I supposed to do, wait here?"

"That's the idea."

"Suppose Indians come around."

"Just talk 'em to death," Ruff said. He was tired of Cherry, and had been for a good long time. "Do you have a gun?" he asked more practically.

"I got one. Always, Justice," Cherry said.

"Good."

Ruff watched Cherry, but he couldn't quite read him. He unbelted his Colt and long knife and slung the belt around his neck and over his shoulder, the Colt across his chest. Then, with a small shake of his head, he went over the side to splash through the waist-deep water to the base of the rising bluff.

The water was dark and still. The bluffs were fluted, deeply shadowed. And Cherry had been right: that sandstone wasn't going to support that much weight. It was crumbling, eroded by time and weather.

He couldn't go back and so he started up.

Ruff reached up and pulled himself slowly from the water. His buckskins were heavy with water and his weight was supported only by one hand gripping a knob of stone, but he managed to pull himself up, wedge a boot into a seam in the bluff, and proceed up a narrow declivity.

He looked straight up, trying to find handholds. Twice in the first minute he had outcroppings crumble beneath his hand, and the second time he nearly went down. He lost his grip, felt the world pull away from him, and it was only by jamming his fist into a crack in the wall of stone that he was able to pull himself forward again to stand hugging the bluff like a suckling child hugging its mother's tit.

He started on again. It was growing dark, the climbing more difficult. The ledge he had seen from below proved to be too narrow to use to make any progress.

Twice he had to climb down to begin again, making only the slowest of progress. He glanced down and saw Cherry far below sitting in the dinghy, his head turned up. Ruff's heart was hammering with the exertion, his breath coming in short gasps. He looked up and started on again, thinking how easy a target his back made for a Sioux warrior or anyone else who wanted him dead—like Cherry? Or Wyatt? Like the sailor with the lead-weight sap, whoever he was? Like Lt. Weeks? Or the major . . . or . . .

He climbed on.

It was the longest hundred feet Ruff had negotiated for some time, but finally he threw a leg up and over and rolled onto the flat above.

The Sioux had been waiting, and now, with a war cry ringing in the air, he charged.

Ruff Justice threw himself back and landed hard on the ground. He yanked the Colt from its holster and fired twice. The first bullet missed the lunging Sioux, but the second tagged meat and bone as the Sioux's war ax swished past Ruff's ear.

The Sioux screamed in pain. His ax struck steel and Ruff's Colt slid away across the ledge.

Justice saw the blood on the warrior's shoulder, saw the pain and savage anger in his eyes, and he clawed at his belt sheath, bringing up his stag-handled bowie as the wounded Sioux swung out wildly with his own knife.

The blades met. Ruff's bowie with its curved blade slashed down and severed a finger on the Sioux's right hand. The man didn't even yell. He was a Sioux; he was a warrior. He was not afraid to be hurt, not afraid to die.

He cut out at Justice, trying to rip his throat open, but Ruff blocked the Sioux's wrist with his forearm and rolled away, coming to his feet to face the wounded warrior as sundown bled across the canyon, painting the many-channeled river orange and gold, shadowing the hills beyond, the islands that appeared to be floating in molten copper.

The Sioux crouched, knife in hand, blade turned up for a disemboweling stroke, watching Ruff with black eyes. Justice glanced toward the brush behind the warrior, the mat of greasewood, sage, chia, and sumac that frosted the bluff, and seeing no sign of arriving help, he focused his attention on the wounded Sioux.

"You're hurt," Ruff told him softly. "You're a young man. You've gotta long life ahead of you. Go now."

The Sioux circled slowly, ignoring Ruff, who repeated it all now in the Sioux tongue. "Go now and live," he said, but the Sioux took it for boasting instead of what it was—real concern, a regret at having to take his life. The young warrior came at Ruff with a yell, knife arcing up toward Justice's gullet.

Ruff stepped back and then in again, his hand locking on the Indian's wrist before a second stroke could be tried. The world went dark and the two men stood together on the sunset-colored bluff, their bodies straining, death glinting in their hands as the knives caught the last rays of the sun.

Ruff's bowie broke free of the injured Sioux's desperate grip and the knife plunged into his chest, entering above the collarbone, the tip severing the aorta, cutting away lung tissue. The Sioux died in seconds, his young eyes wide, frightened at last. Ruff let him go and he fell from the bluff to splash into the dark water beside Cherry's boat.

Cherry looked up in shock and grabbed for his concealed pistol, but it was over. The young warrior floated facedown in the dark, gently moving water, and Ruff Justice stood silhouetted against the sunset atop the bluff.

Ruff had time to map the river in his mind before the sun was fully down. He could see the main channel break free and swing around toward the east, where it would rejoin the Missouri. He followed it back to its improbable beginning beyond a small oak-covered island, and then he started back down in the near darkness.

He moved very carefully, climbing by feel more than sight. He made it halfway and then the rock beneath his hand crumbled away and he had to launch himself backward, pushing away from the bluff that fell after him in a shower of stone and dust.

It might not have been a pretty dive, but it did the job. The back dive ended abruptly in the cold, dark water. Ruff turned his body, knowing it had to be shallow. His hands scraped bottom, jolting him to the shoulder joints, but he didn't do himself any permanent damage. When he came up, Cherry was standing in the boat, peering into the water with expectation.

"Sorry—I'm alive," Ruff said, after wiping back his hair. He dragged himself up and into the dinghy. "Let's get back to the *Jacksonville* while we can still see."

They were waiting. Sally Shore looked him up and down and grunted. "Learn anything?"

Nancy Hawkins made a bit more of a fuss. "God, Justice, we saw you fall . . . We all thought you were a goner." And she threw her arms around his neck, holding him tight for a long moment, her tears warm against his cheek. Sally made a disgusted noise.

"Well? I asked you, Justice, did you learn anything?"

"We'll make it out," he said, and she relaxed visibly, her taut nerves letting her become human once again.

"You'll bet on that?" she asked cautiously.

"I'll bet on it."

He would have bet on several other points. They weren't yet through with the Sioux, for one thing. Nor were they rid of the troublemaker who had wrecked the engine with a sledgehammer. Nor had they even begun to have trouble with Griff Oakland—there was too much at stake here.

It wasn't the time to mention any of that.

"I'll bet on it," he said, and he gave Sally Shore a wink and a smile, which she accepted with a slight, hesitant smile of her own. In the darkness somewhere an owl hooted and the river went dark. The Sioux were moving around. The river had become a black, desolate place, and Sally Shore was suddenly scared. Anyone who wasn't scared was probably insane.

"Issue arms, Cherry," Sally said. "This might be a long, long night."

7

Ruff Justice had had first watch, so he was in his bunk when his cabin door opened at midnight. He sat up, Colt lifting to point toward the rectangle of star-spattered blue-black sky that marked the doorway.

"Better back on out," Ruff said quietly, but then his eyes picked up the soft curves of a female body and he lowered his gun. "Nancy," he said, shaking his head. "Listen, honey, I like you. You're a fine-looking woman, but you're just too young for me . . ."

"Good." Sally Shore slipped into the cabin. "I'm glad to hear you admit it."

"Sally?"

"Yes . . . Sally. All that touching and kissing and poking you're always doing—have you got a little of it for me, tall man?" She hesitated. "Maybe I shouldn't be here."

Ruff lay back and held the blanket up, and Sally crossed the room to slip in beside him, naked and warm. She lay with her head on his chest for a long while, just listening to his heartbeat.

"If you really . . ." she began, lifting her head.

"Oh, shut up, Sally Shore," Justice said, and rolled her onto her side, kissing her lips, her throat, as her fingers clutched at his back with tiny uneasy, eager movements.

Her lips parted as Ruff's mouth met hers, and with a satisfied sigh she wrapped her arms around him and slowly lifted her knees, allowing Justice to slip between them.

Her breasts were full and warm, the nipples taut as Ruff's lips roved across them. Sally stroked his long dark hair and then reached between his legs, touching him, positioning him quickly. Ruff arched his back a little and slid home and Sally locked her ankles behind him.

"It's good, isn't it?" Sally said. "It's been so long I'd nearly forgotten how good."

Ruff pushed it home, his pelvis nudging hers. Sally's eyes were lighted by the thin band of moonlight that fell through the slatted cabin door. Her face looked softened, pleasured, feminine, much different from the captain's face she usually wore. She began to respond now, her hips lifting, her body altering, softening, growing damp and heavy as she lazily raised her body and clutched at him, her inner muscles gripping Ruff, urging him on.

Ruff's hands roamed her breasts, slipped beneath her, and clenched her smooth, muscular buttocks, feeling the warmth and pulse of her body, eager now, ready, ripe, wanting one more nudge, one stroke to split open like a sweet rich fruit.

Sally breathed softly, quickly, in cadence. Her breath was against Ruff's throat, her fingers probed him, reached for him, wondered at him as he lifted himself and buried himself in her. She began to shudder and Ruff saw her mouth open like a woman in pain.

She clung to his neck, her arms warm and strong. Her body lifted against his, pitching, swaying, rolling frantically, striving toward a need she had nearly forgotten. When she found it, she released her breath in a sharp gasp and she trembled, losing control of her body. It was like an uncaged animal wanting to devour Ruff Justice.

He let it. He rode the swaying, the bucking of her body and clung to her, feeling his own need rise and then flow out of him in a sudden hard climax.

Sally was still, utterly still. Then slowly her hands began their stroking again, moving up his spine to his neck, where light fingers rubbed the long muscles beneath his dark hair. She touched his ears, his shoulder blades, his hard-muscled thighs in wonder. After a while she began to hum very softly.

"Who was he?" Ruff asked. The hand that had been stroking his back stopped its motion.

"Who?"

"The man you lost," Ruff said.

"Hell of a time to talk about it."

"Then don't."

"Tact. I thought you had none—I was right."

"I said don't talk about it, Sally. I just wondered, that's all."

"Why would you wonder?"

"Because I care for you."

"Me?" She laughed.

"Sure. I like you but I feel like you're not showing me all of yourself. And so I wondered. I don't like secrets."

She sighed deeply. Her mouth was beside his ear. He could hear the small hesitant breaths she took before she actually began speaking.

"His name was Joe Jolly. A sailor. Who else would I meet? He was young and hard and he grinned a lot. The girls all liked him, but I liked him best, I suppose. Anyway, I pursued him the hardest. I made a fool out of myself, I know I did. So what? What's love if not making a fool out of yourself? I knew I wanted Joe Jolly, so I went to get him. What's hanging back get you?"

"Seldom much," Ruff answered.

"That's right." She had gotten herself a little worked up. Now she took a slower, deeper breath and continued. "So we were going to get married . . . we put it off once and then again. My fault. I'd just bought the *Jacksonville* and I wanted to get her on a paying basis. One more trip to St. Louis."

"Where was Jolly?"

"Working for Cap MacAdoo. On the old *Birmingham.*"

"The one that sank."

"The one that sank. In that storm one terrible night. I recall the storm so well. It came down the river, roaring and stamping and threatening, and we started to get waves up ten, twelve feet. Wind waves. We were set for a hurricane, looked like. We tied up hard and sat to wait it out. Lightning—God, you never seen lightning like that, carving figures in the sky, and the thunder was never-ending."

Sally Shore went on, "Suddenly I knew. I was sitting there in the wheelhouse wondering how Jolly was making it on the *Birmingham*, knowing he was a good pilot, but still wondering, when suddenly I knew: he was dead."

"Was he?"

"Yes." She sniffled and something warm and damp touched Ruff's cheek. "He went down with the *Birmingham*, and that was that. That was just that—too bad for Jolly, too bad for Sally Shore."

Ruff didn't say anything. There isn't much you can say at such a time. He just held her a little tighter and lay with her as the moon drifted over and the night slowly passed away.

Ruff was slow in rising. The throbbing of the engines and the whispering hiss of the relief valves brought him awake and to his feet. He rubbed his head and sat staring at the gray morning outside. It was cool and damp. The smells of stagnant water, decomposing vegetation, and river fog mingled and drifted coldly through his cabin.

His buckskins were still wet. He put on his spare jeans and a deep-red shirt with white bone buttons. He belted on his Colt after cleaning it and changing the loads, and went up on deck in time to feel the

Jacksonville give a little lurch and begin its slow backing motion.

Sally told him, "I was just coming to get you. You're the only one who knows where we're going." She paused for a moment, smiled, and touched his arm, and then became the captain again.

Justice said, "Let's go up and I'll try to show you on your charts."

Cap was easing the *Jacksonville* away from the dead-end channel. He waved a hand to Ruff. His pipe smoked away merrily in his mouth. Sally got the charts out again.

"No," Ruff said, "you can't see much on here. Half the channels don't exist, according to this. Not surprising. We have to go back to the main channel, take the second arm to the right, follow it for about a mile or so—it bends a lot, Cap, but stick with it. Then we come to an island that has a twin oak on it and nothing else. If we swing east again there, we're home free. We'll come out on a big lake. Then it should be clear sailing into Fort Union," he finished.

"And we should be well ahead of Griff Oakland."

"With any luck."

"We haven't found the first channel yet," Cap said cautiously.

"We will." Sally had confidence enough for the three of them. "We'll find it and we'll get to Union ahead of Griff Oakland. That's just about the half-way point, isn't it? What can stop us then?"

"The other half," Ruff said under his breath. If this had seemed difficult, Justice knew that they hadn't even seen wild river yet. They had Fort Union to try fueling at, making any repairs, procuring supplies. After Union there was nothing at all for three hundred miles. Fort Peck had been closed down abruptly by the Sioux the year before. Above Union no steam vessel had ever sailed, and damn few white-built boats of any kind. They were moving deeper into the Sioux heartland, and that didn't mean a few reservation-jumpers, it meant Red Cloud's armies. There was that, and also Griff Oakland, who was as mad as Sally to attempt this, who would apparently let nothing stand in his way.

And on board the *Jacksonville* there was a saboteur and a would-be killer.

"There it is!" Cap called out. "There's the channel."

Sally let out a little yip and threw her arms around Justice's neck. Then, blushing, she got back to her work. Ruff got back to his worrying.

They wound for most of the morning through the airless forest of reeds and cattails. Dark gloomy oaks like something deep in the South overhung the channels. The *Jacksonville*, like a great creature in a forgotten place, sluggishly roamed the waterways, backing, finding new courses until at midafternoon she broke free and steamed out onto the broad, silver bright lake.

"Open her up, Cap," Sally shouted. "Open that throttle."

Cap did, and the engines, which had sounded sluggish, unsure, wary, now seemed to rejoice and stretch iron muscles and roar with newfound strength as the *Jacksonville* steamed onto the wide lake.

Farley Wyatt found Ruff dozing on the texas deck, sitting on a bale of regulation army trousers, his back against the sun-warmed wall.

Justice's eyes were closed; he appeared to be sound asleep. A borrowed straw hat shaded his face. He was slack, as relaxed as a cat. But like a cat, he was not as sound asleep as he seemed. Farley saw a blue eye wink open.

"What is it, Wyatt?"

"Mad at me?" Wyatt sat down beside Ruff, removing his hat.

"Why should I be?"

"No reason. Say, Justice, what have they got at this Fort Union? That's the next stop, isn't it?"

"That's right, Fort Union."

"Is there a town there, I mean? Stage transportation or some such."

"Planning on jumping ship?"

"I don't know. Maybe so."

Ruff studied the young man, decided he was lying, and answered. "There's nothing there but the fort and a trading post. A small Indian settlement."

"Damn." Farley Wyatt looked across the gleaming lake into the distances. "Well, that's that. I guess I'm stuck."

"All the way to Benton—if we get there."

"Is it that bad?"

"It's that bad," Ruff replied.

"Damn," Wyatt said again.

He rose, put his hat on, and left without ever having told Justice what it was he was really after. Ruff shrugged it away. He had enough to occupy his mind.

He heard some excited yelling on the upper deck and he uncoiled, coming to his feet. He saw Cherry pointing southward and he peered that way into the sunlight, brilliant off the lake. He saw nothing—until he got to the upper deck himself, swinging up over the brass-mounted rail.

The *River Nymph* was back there, chugging away, steaming toward the *Jacksonville*. She hadn't fallen far behind despite Sally's shortcut. The time the *Jacksonville* had spent broken down had kept things fairly even.

"He was running the lake last night," Cap MacAdoo guessed. "It's wide enough to allow it."

Behind was Griff Oakland, and now, slowly rising from the shore ahead was a dark stain, a row of jumbled cubes against the green of the surrounding country—Fort Union.

"If he's got any sense, he won't put in to Union," Sally said savagely. "Because if he does, and I get the chance, I'll kill Griff Oakland, so help me I will. He tried to wreck the *Jacksonville.*"

"Easy, Sally," Ruff said. "We don't know it was him."

"Who else could have been behind it?"

"I don't know. But don't talk yourself into a corner. He's got to put in to Union and you know it. It's the last chance for supplies and cut wood between here and Benton."

"I know. Nerves." Her fingers touched her forehead and she smiled weakly. Then her confidence came booming back. "Take us in, Cap!" she yelled, and the whistle tooted twice as the *Jacksonville* swung toward Fort Union.

They tied up in the shade of some huge spruce trees that had grown up crooked and overhung the dock. It seemed that, before now, the dock had been used only by flatboats and Indian canoes. The piny scent was fresh and clean, welcome.

"You know the commander of this fort?" Sally asked.

"Hodges? Yes, but he won't want to see me."

"You've had words?"

"We've had a little more than that. You'd better see him by yourself if you're hoping to come by some wood."

Sally wondered briefly what it was that Hodges and Justice had collided over, but Justice offered no explanation and she put her mind to work on other things.

The whistle on the *River Nymph* sounded three times, reaching them distinctly across the flat, calm surface of the big lake. Sally's mouth tightened. With Lydell Cherry at her shoulder, she started off toward the fort, which was surrounded by spruce and pine.

Ruff watched them weave through the trees. Then, positioning his borrowed straw hat, he started toward the trading post.

* * *

LaCroix had been the Frenchman's name, and he had come into the big country when there were no white faces for five hundred miles. He had taken a wife, an Ojibwa woman, and built his trading post on the river. He had introduced the Sioux to steel knives and powder-and-ball weapons. And rum. They had a lot of rum to drink one night and decided that steel knives and powder-and-ball weapons should be given to them instead of traded for furs. LaCroix had disagreed, but it hadn't done him much good.

They scalped the Frenchman and left him, still alive, hanging by a rope strung through the big tendons behind his heels, upside down beneath a big pine. The wolves had started at his face and eaten their way up. The Ojibwa had been taken away and she had married a Sioux warrior with six toes on both feet. They drank much rum and one night the Ojibwa woman stabbed the Sioux to death in drunken anger.

They were all gone, but the trading post remained. Ruff could see it now through the trees. He was a hundred yards from it when Lt. John Lewis Weeks stepped from behind a big pine, a pistol in his hand. The pistol, unfortunately, was leveled at Ruff's guts.

"Just hold it." The kid's hand was shaking, but that only made him more dangerous. A trembling finger had no place on the trigger of an army revolver.

"What's the problem, Weeks?"

"I think you know what it is."

"Let's pretend I don't."

The kid walked nearer. His face was the color of candle wax. The hand still trembled. "I'll kill you if you move."

"I'm not moving."

Weeks looked up the wooded path toward the dock, then back sharply to Ruff. "You were warned. You should have left her alone."

"Left who alone?"

"Nancy! Do you think I'm stupid?"

One doesn't answer a question like that. Ruff stood watching the young officer, his hands raised. Weeks' eyes looked as if he had been hitting the bottle.

"Major Hawkins prod you into this?" Ruff asked.

"No one has to tell me what's right."

"No? It looks like someone has to tell you right and wrong. What's on your mind, kid? Nancy? There's nothing between us. She's a pretty young woman. I like seeing her, talking to her. That's all there is to it."

"Don't lie!" Weeks exploded.

"All right, I won't."

"Maybe I'm young, but I think I know when a woman's been with a man. You can see it in their eyes, smell it, sense it."

"Fine. It wasn't me. I think you've been put up to this. Was it the major?"

"No!" Weeks said in a way that indicated it almost certainly was.

"Have you talked to Nancy about this?"

Weeks shook his head. "I don't have to talk to her."

"No? I see. You just get suspicions planted in your little brain and you go out looking for someone to kill. I don't like that, Weeks. It shows a lack of mental competence. What I like less is you choosing me, coming here and waving a gun in my face for something that's basically none of your damned business."

"It's my business—we're going to get married."

"Have you asked her?"

"Not directly." The young officer looked confused. But the gun in his hand was as purposeful as ever.

"Why don't you? Afraid she might refuse? Afraid of women in general, Nancy in particular? You want her but haven't got the guts to try getting her? You butter up Major Hawkins and try to get through to his daughter that way? Is that it?"

"Shut up!" Weeks' lip curled back with genuine

rage, the first real emotion Ruff had seen in this confused young man. "You think you're something. You think the women fall over themselves trying to get to you."

"I don't think anything. Two people want each other or they don't, that's all."

"And you wanted Nancy; Nancy wanted you."

"Not that much, or we'd be together," Ruff said.

"And you were! Last night. Someone saw her leaving your cabin."

"It wasn't Nancy."

"Who, then? Who else *is* there?"

"None of your damned business."

Weeks said, "You're lying to me, Justice."

"I don't like that—I never will. I can't get used to people calling me a liar. I don't lie."

"You are lying now."

"Am I?"

"She was seen, I tell you," Weeks said almost pleadingly.

"The hell she was. Not leaving my cabin."

"She wasn't in her own."

Ruff shook his head. "That's nothing to do with me, Weeks."

"It was you. I'm going to kill you for it."

"Murder for love?" Ruff said. "Romantic but stupid."

"You'll have a chance. Choose your weapons."

"*Suicide* for love—well, that's a grand tradition, too," Ruff Justice said sarcastically.

"Don't make sport of me, damn you!"

"No." Ruff was suddenly deadly earnest. "I won't make sport of you. I don't joke about someone dying. I just wanted to let you know what I thought of the idea. I wanted to tell you that you are wrong. I wanted to tell you no man calls me a liar twice."

Weeks said very slowly, "You are a liar."

"You have a knife?" Ruff asked.

"Why?"

"Because you offered me a choice of weapons. That's what I'm going to use. Knives. It's a little different than a gun. You have to feel the bowels, the blood leak onto your hand. You have to hold your adversary close while he dies in your arms, praying to God, cursing, calling out for his lover."

"You don't scare me."

"No." Ruff arched one eyebrow. "That's too bad. That means you're even younger and dumber than I thought. If the idea of having a knife tear your guts out doesn't scare you, Lieutenant Weeks, it should. Unless you're utterly mad. What do you say?"

"I've got a knife," was his answer.

8

Weeks had a knife. Ruff Justice had one too. What Weeks didn't know was that the knife Justice carried had killed a dozen men, several of them in duels fought in the Cajun style, with two men's wrists strapped together. He also didn't know that the last thing in the world Ruff felt like doing was killing a young army officer for being infatuated with a pretty young woman.

They stepped off the path and walked a little way into the woods. A jay scolded them. Distantly a crow cawed. The sky was a deep blue through the tall pines. Ruff was growing angry.

He couldn't envision himself as immortal, and he knew that when guns started firing or deadly steel flashing, anyone can die. Maybe he was better than Weeks, but it didn't mean a thing. One cut across the throat, the arteries at the wrist, on the thigh, and Justice could slowly bleed to death while the crow kept on cawing.

"This is some sort of damned foolishness, Weeks."

"It's honor."

"Very honorable. Very damned foolish. Now can we forget it—you've proven you're a man."

"There's got to be blood, Justice."

Ruff stopped and faced Weeks across a small, pine-needle-strewn clearing. "I'll tell you once more I wasn't with Nancy Hawkins last night."

"I'll tell you once again you're a liar," Weeks said, and he was so scared he was trembling. His tallow-colored face was frozen into a mock rictus.

He had a rosewood-handled knife in his hand, balancing it, testing its weight. Ruff Justice breathed a curse and drew his big bowie.

Behind the trees men were walking toward the trading post, talking loudly, singing. They had to be the *River Nymph*'s crew. Most of them would live out the day. One of those in the clearing likely wouldn't.

"All right, Weeks, let's have at it." Justice began to circle, trying to plan his tactics toward disabling the young officer without killing him. It wasn't his fault he was young, dumb, pushed into this by Maj. Hawkins.

Weeks slashed out awkwardly with his knife. The blade came too close to Ruff's face for comfort. Justice decided maybe he was carrying benevolence too far.

"I don't want to do it, Weeks."

"Then stand still, damn you, and let me have your blood."

Weeks had gone crazy with fear. He wanted to strike out, to kill before he could be harmed. He cut out wildly with his knife, backing Ruff up. Justice had it in mind to try for the fingers, maybe the tendons inside the right elbow. It would cripple Weeks for life, ruin his new career, but it beat killing or being killed.

The gunshots from the trading post broke the fight off as sharply as a twig being snapped. Weeks looked at Ruff and both men started running toward LaCroix's old post. They burst out of the trees together and saw the beginnings of the melee.

Later they were told how it started. A man from the *Jacksonville* reached for a plug of tobacco paid for by a man from the *River Nymph*, thinking it was the plug he had purchased. With both crews ready to go off like a powder keg, that was all it took.

Someone fired a gun into the ceiling and the two parties came together like opposing armies reduced to hand-to-hand combat.

Emerging from the trees at a dead run, Ruff saw Curly, his old friend from downriver, slam his fist into the face of a *Jacksonville* crewman, knocking him over the log rail around the trading-post porch.

Curly turned and was kicked in the stomach by Farley Wyatt. The kick slammed him back against the log wall of the trading post and Curly sagged down to sit on the porch staring at nothing, out cold.

Inside the mayhem was complete. Ruff fought his way across the porch and inside by slugging a *River Nymph* man in the neck, kicking another on the kneecap. Within, a flour barrel flew across the room and exploded against the far wall like a white bomb. A huge sailor with a massive chest and heavily tattooed forearms looked around for something else to throw.

Griff Oakland was suddenly in Ruff's way and Justice found a target that appealed to him a lot more than the green army lieutenant. Oakland recognized Ruff as well and pushed his sleeves up.

"Come on, scout. Let's have at it." Stubby fingers gestured Ruff in. In a moment Oakland had second thoughts. Ruff feinted with a left and then smashed Oakland's lips and nose flat with a stinging right-hand shot. Oakland backed away and hit the counter behind him, spilling cans of molasses, blankets, belts, and boots.

He came to his feet with a roar and moved in on Justice. Ruff backed away, jabbing, keeping Oakland off him. From the corner of his eyes Justice saw someone with a chair overhead step toward him. He ducked and kicked out sideways, catching the man in the groin. The chair came down anyway and rapped Ruff's shoulder painfully, striking the nerve cluster there, momentarily paralyzing that arm. Ruff backed away, fighting one-handed.

Oakland was smiling now with his split and bloodied mouth. He had Justice and knew it. He threw a savage right that caught Ruff flush and jolted him to his heels. Ruff pawed at Oakland with his good arm, tried to duck away, and took another right to the jaw.

Justice had his head moving away as it landed, but it still stung. Oakland had muscle in his shoulders and purpose in his eyes—he meant to beat the hell out of someone from the *Jacksonville* and he had his man.

Or so he thought.

Ruff Justice had other ideas. He tipped over a chair in Oakland's path as he backed away, feeling the pain in his shoulder intensify, not diminish, tasting blood in his mouth.

Oakland kicked the chair aside and came on stolidly. Behind Ruff someone went down with a groan of pain as an ax handle met a sailor's hard skull.

Ruff could see the open door from the corner of his eye, see Lydell Cherry and Sally coming on the run, with them a man in uniform. Capt. Hodges, the post commander, Ruff thought.

Oakland had him backed into the corner now and he moved in close to try some body punching. Ruff dropped his elbows and covered up, dropping his face between his fists.

"Here's one for you, scout," Oakland grunted, and he unleashed a right hand shot to Ruff's ribs. "Here's another:" The left landed on the other side just behind the liver.

Justice waited, rolling slightly from side to side as Oakland laid on all he had. He took the punches from the *River Nymph*'s captain and bided his time, letting the feeling come back into his arm, letting Oakland punch himself arm-weary.

When Ruff came out of his crouch, he was like lightning let out of a jug. Two lefts struck so quickly that Oakland never saw them. A right uppercut snapped the big mate's head back, cracking the teeth in front, spraying Ruff with blood. Oakland gave a little inarticulate cry and stepped back, hands fumbling for Ruff's shirtfront.

Justice hit him again, on the ear this time, and Oakland staggered sideways clumsily, walking right into Ruff Justice's left-hand hook. Oakland went down. Like a bull bison clipped through the spine with a big-grained bullet, he went down cold, thumped against the wooden floor of the trading post, and stayed there, white eyes looking at nothing, his breathing ragged, fast.

"Look out, Justice!"

Ruff turned at the warning from Lydell Cherry and saw the man with the ax handle descending on him. Justice kicked out savagely at the man's belly and drove him back and into Cherry's arms.

The big mate spun the sailor, gripped the ax handle with one hand, and drove his fist into his face. The man with the ax handle went down, leaving Cherry to wield his weapon. Near the door Farley Wyatt had tangled with a dark, Indian-looking man. He seemed to be holding his own. Ruff saw Farley stab two lefts into the man's face, hook with a right, block a kick at his groin, and hit the Indian again, hard enough to drive him out the door and onto the porch of the trading post, where a small group of soldiers was trying ineffectually to restore order.

The man with the knife was behind Lt. Weeks, who should have known better than to get involved in this. Ruff saw the malicious grin on the sailor's face as he threw his arm around Weeks' throat and drove the knife up toward the officer's spine.

It never got there. Ruff was beside the firebox and he snatched up a length of wood, bringing it down solidly on the sailor's wrist. Bone cracked and the man howled with pain, falling away from Weeks, who turned panting, red-faced.

"Thanks . . ." Then he saw who it was. "That doesn't mean a thing, Justice. We still have an appointment."

"You're welcome." Ruff nodded toward the back door. "Get the hell out of here. What's it going to look like with an officer and a gentleman brawling in here?"

Weeks started to argue automatically, then glanced toward the front of the trading post, where Capt. Hodges was ordering his men to use as much force as necessary to break it up.

Weeks nodded and went out, hatless.

Ruff Justice found a corner chair and sat down. The fight was over. There was just a little mopping up to do, and the soldiers did that with fair efficiency.

The sailors were grabbed and turned toward the door. Those who objected were prodded along with rifles—bayonets attached. In five minutes there were only two bleeding, moaning men on the floor of the ravaged trading post and, sitting in the corner, his legs crossed at the knee, Ruff Justice.

The soldiers crossed the room, their boots kicking up puffs of flour dust. On their heels was Capt. Hodges, who winced as he saw Justice. Behind the officer was Sally Shore.

"I might have known," was what Hodges said.

"Hello, Captain."

"I might have known when I heard there was a riot going on at the trading post that it was either drunk Indians or Ruffin T. Justice. Arrest this man."

"Captain, I know Mister Justice didn't start this." Sally Shore stepped around the soldiers to face Hodges. "Did you, Ruff?"

"No."

"He was involved."

"So were most of my men. Are you going to arrest my entire crew?"

Hodges looked as if he would like to, but he thought it over and shook his head. "I suppose not. Go on, get him out of here. Then you get your wood and supplies and get upriver. Before you go, however, I want you and the other captain, wherever he is, to have this place cleaned up and pay for any damage."

"Yes, sir," Sally said briskly. Then she hurriedly grabbed Ruff's arm and practically yanked him to his feet, guiding him out of the trading post. "You didn't have to antagonize him," she said once they were outside, walking swiftly toward the river.

"I didn't think I was. Besides, it doesn't take anything for Hodges to get worked up."

"You *didn't* start that, did you?" Sally asked, stopping to face Ruff.

"No, I was busy fighting a duel with Lieutenant Weeks. I was just stupid enough to get sucked into it." He started away again and Sally yanked him to her.

"Wait a minute—you slid on past something there, Ruffin. What do you mean you were fighting a duel with Lieutenant Weeks?"

"Just what I said."

"With guns?"

"Knives, actually."

Sally looked exasperated and a little scared. "But why? Over Nancy Hawkins?"

"He thought so. Actually, it was over you."

"What do you mean, Justice? Are you always this mysterious?"

"I mean that someone saw you leaving my cabin this morning and they told Weeks it was Nancy Hawkins."

"Damn all! It wasn't, was it, Ruff?"

"Now who's mysterious? What do you mean?"

"It wasn't Nancy Hawkins—after I left, maybe?"

"Do you think I'm insatiable, woman?"

"I have considered it, yes."

Ruff put an arm around her shoulders and drew her nearer. "No." He spoke very slowly. "It wasn't Nancy Hawkins."

"Then why didn't you tell Weeks it was me? Send him to me—I'll tell him."

"It didn't seem real gentlemanly, Sally."

She laughed harshly and shook her head. "*Damn* gentlemanly! You'd rather die than tell Weeks it was me testing your bunk with you last night?" A second thought entered her mind. "Maybe you were ashamed to tell him."

"That," Ruff said with considerable firmness, "was the farthest thing from my mind and you know it, Sally Shore."

"You mean it?"

"You know I do. You know you're a fine-looking woman and you can raise my blood pressure without any trouble."

"Really?" Her eyes had softened. She was next to him, looking up at him.

"Really." He kissed her briefly before approaching footsteps caused Sally to step hastily back.

She straightened her hat and waved a careless hand. "Well, all right, Mister Justice, I'll talk to you later."

"Ashamed of me or something?" Ruff cracked.

Sally flushed. She looked at the three approaching sailors and moved to Justice again. She kissed him full on the lips, deeply, and then smiled at him. The sailors gawked and spoke in snickering whispers as they went past.

"Satisfied?" she asked.

"Yes."

"But it's bad for discipline." She glanced after her sailors. "Very bad for discipline."

When Ruff reached the dock with Sally, the sailors were already loading wood. Most of the men had a swollen jaw or scabbed forehead.

"I've got to get into the strongbox, Ruff. There's damages to pay for."

Justice nodded and watched as she climbed the gangplank. He turned at the sound of a familiar, obnoxious voice. Maj. Hawkins, half-supported by his daughter, was weaving his way toward the boat.

"Damnedest thing," he said, slurring the words rather badly. "A captain! Snubs me like that."

Apparently Hodges hadn't welcomed the major with open arms. Ruff couldn't blame the man. The major had had about six too many.

"Need any help, Nancy?"

Maj. Hawkins' head snapped up. "No help from a bastard like you."

"No, thank you," Nancy said, looking at Ruff with helpless eyes. "We're going to make it."

"Damn right," the major chimed in, "going to make it. Why wouldn't we make it to damned boat?"

Ruff stepped aside, his mouth tightening. The major was killing himself and hurting Nancy. The army wouldn't tolerate this long; a drink now and then was one thing, but this was more than that. It was constant, habitual drunkenness and it was no state for a field officer to be in when his decisions could cost men's lives.

Sally was on deck, waving an arm. Ruff walked to where she stood displaying an empty metal box.

"Gone," she said.

"What?"

"The money, it's gone. Someone's gotten into the cash box."

Ruff took the metal box. The scratches around the lock made it clear someone had jimmied it open. He frowned. "Who knew where it was?"

"Just about anyone on the crew," she answered, touching her forehead nervously. "Ruff, I need that money now. I have to pay for this wood. Hodges didn't give it to us. It was purchased from the trader. He'll demand it back."

"Then we'll cut our own."

"By that time"—she lifted her chin—"the *River Nymph* will be long gone. We caught her this time.

We were lucky. We can't continue to run behind her and hope to beat Oakland to Fort Benton."

"No." Ruff took a slow breath. "How much is it?"

"Have you got any money?" Her eyes widened excitedly.

"Mercenary lady."

"When I *need* it."

"No, I don't have it." Sally's face fell. "But," he added quickly, "I may be able to get it."

"How?"

"I'm army personnel. I can try borrowing against my back pay. They can charge it to Fort Lincoln somehow. If they want to, it can't be that complicated."

"But Captain Hodges—"

"You don't know the army, do you? Captain Hodges doesn't know half of what's going on on this post, in his own office—I'll promise you that. If he's got a sharp head clerk and a good first sergeant, he doesn't need to know. He doesn't care to know. The commander's not supposed to be bothered by all these small problems." Ruff winked.

"You think you can swing it, really?" Sally Shore asked.

"I think so. If Sergeant Crook is still here."

She threw arms around her neck.

Ruff grinned. "I haven't got it yet. Besides, Sally, this is awful bad for discipline." He stepped back, still grinning, and headed off toward the fort, his stride long, confident. Sally watched him go, standing with her fingers crossed behind her back.

Sgt. Crook was still there. A big jovial man with a Swedish accent belying his assumed name and identity, he had supposedly killed his wife's lover with his bare hands, and the story was easy to believe. Crook was a massive man; seeing him without his shirt was enough to pale strong, war-hardened soldiers. He had no discipline problems with subordinates whatsoever. He smiled as Ruff came in and stood to shake hands.

"Roof," he said, "it is so good to see you again. Not since the Milk River, hey?"

"Not since then. How's things?"

"Everyt'ing is beautiful. Quiet. No killing the Indians."

"Good to hear it." Ruff went ahead then and told Crook what he needed.

The sergeant nodded understanding. "Not'ing to worry. I'll give it you out of the company fund. You pay me back from Lincoln."

"Maybe we'd better make firmer arrangements," Ruff said.

"Oh?" Crook pursed his lips. "You t'ink maybe you not get back to Lincoln."

"There's always a chance, isn't there?"

"Ya. Always a chance. Okay. I have the clerk write up a voucher."

And that was the way it was done. Fifteen minutes later Ruff left the orderly room without having seen Hodges, and in his pocket were fifty gold dollars.

He met Lt. Weeks on the way and cursed his luck, but the young officer hadn't come to fight this time. Shamefaced, he apologized. "I talked to Captain Shore. Rather, she talked to me—marched up and told me off. It was humiliating . . . She told me who it was leaving your cabin. Humiliating . . ." Weeks shook his head and smiled crookedly. "What an ass I was."

"You let Major Hawkins talk you into it?"

"I guess I did."

"Want some cheap advice? Stay away from him as much as possible. He's going down and he'll take you with him. His judgment isn't worth a damn."

"He's going to be my commanding officer."

"Yes, and he's Nancy's father. That doesn't make him infallible, nor does it mean you owe him more than military courtesy."

"Yes, but—"

"Yes, but he nearly got you killed. Protecting his

daughter like he is. Selling her to you. Wanting to choose her road."

"I know that, I guess I know it now."

"Killing someone isn't going to make her love you, Weeks."

"No." Color spotted the kid's cheeks. "I guess it isn't, but if I find out who it is, I'll kill him anyway and the consequences be damned. I mean that. I'm apologizing to you because you're the wrong man, Justice, not because I'm ashamed of challenging a man to a duel over Nancy. I'd do it again," he said, and he added grimly, "and it looks like I will." Then Weeks turned and walked away through the shade of the pines.

Justice watched him until he was out of sight. Son, Ruff said to himself, you are begging someone to kill you. Keep begging and it's going to happen.

9

It was nearly dusk when they set out from Fort Union. Too late to sail, but the *River Nymph* made her move and Sally cast lines off, opened the throttles, and set off in pursuit, running upriver as orange streaked the evening skies and the water went to dark silk.

They made good time, twenty miles before nightfall, when both boats anchored in midstream within sight but not hailing distance of each other. Sally posted an armed watch.

"They'll not wreck my engines again," she said.

Ruff didn't bother to point out that it was very unlikely that Griff Oakland's people could have done that particular job, that it had to have been someone on board the *Jacksonville*, a passenger or crewman.

Darkness settled quickly and the river went soft and silent. The moon rose late. Silver, bright, and round, it cast plenty of light for the pirates.

Ruff was sleeping in his cabin when he heard the small scuffling sound on deck. He was awake and alert an instant later, his pistol in hand. He had nearly convinced himelf that it was nothing when he heard another sound—rapid, light footsteps.

Justice pulled on his boots and his buckskin pants and slipped out of the cabin.

He could see the moon above the oaks, the silver-streaked water, and nothing else. Which was wrong, since there should have been a sentry walking the deck. He lifted his eyes toward the *River Nymph*, but couldn't make it out. Oakland had moved his boat. Steaming ahead under the cover of night? Why not? The river was wide, the moon shining . . .

They hit Justice hard. From behind, arms were wrapped around him and a jolting blow landed behind his ear. His knees gave out and he felt himself being half-dragged, half-pushed toward the rail.

He tried to fight back but his arms were pinned. His head flashed with colored lights, hummed with distant, meaningless sounds.

"Dump him, come on. Troll's waiting," he heard one of them say. There was more, but it faded away into a long tunnel filled with crooked little faces.

He came starkly alert suddenly, but it was too late. He was thrown over the rail of the *Jacksonville*, into the inky water, which sucked him down into a cold bottomless pit.

Swim! A voice way back in the recesses of his mind shouted insistently, trying to be heard above the racket of the hundreds of little crooked faces crying out.

Swim! Ruff's eyes opened wide and he realized abruptly just what was happening. He was half-conscious, drowning in the Upper Missouri as the moon shined on the water and the dark trees onshore floated past as he drifted downriver. He gasped, coughed on some water, and tried to paddle toward the bank. He couldn't make it, knew he couldn't. He rolled onto his back and floated, trying to clear his head, waiting for the numbness of mind and body to drift away.

He could see nothing. The world was dark. Dark and liquid and cold. Ruff realized he had closed his eyes, realized he had nearly passed out again. He shook his hair free of his eyes and tried treading water. It was exhausting. Every time he breathed, he breathed in water. The moon was a very funny silver hole in the sky.

Swim! The little voice wouldn't be still. Justice obeyed it finally, stroking cleanly toward the shore. It took intense concentration; his mind still refused to focus properly, his body to obey simple commands.

He drifted farther downriver. How far? He could see nothing of the *Jacksonville*. When he finally dragged himself ashore, he sat for long minutes on a slab of rock, coughing up water, staring at nothing as the night and the river went by.

How long he sat there he didn't know, but the moon was high when the flickering patterns in his mind began to fit themselves together coherently.

The *Jacksonville*. Someone had taken over the boat and thrown him overboard. He recalled a voice near him saying, "Dump him. Troll's waiting."

Ruff was on his feet staring upriver, seeing nothing. Jack Troll had taken the *Jacksonville*.

Troll was a well-known river pirate. Everyone knew about him, but no one, the army included, had been able to stop him. He was the law on the river in this area. Trappers flatboating furs downriver were his prey. His eyes must have glittered with greedy pleasure when he saw those steamboats moor on his stretch of water, knowing that they carried wealth beyond his experience as a river robber baron.

Ruff wiped back his hair with both hands. He was unarmed but for the skinning knife in his boot. He wore only his boots and his sodden buckskin pants.

Troll had many men, many guns. He hadn't survived this long by being careless or merciful. He had the *Jacksonville* and Sally Shore, and there wasn't any reasonable way Ruff Justice could expect to take them away from Troll.

Fort Union was behind him, to the south. He could go down there, get some dry clothes, fill a soft bunk until Troll set Sally free, as he would eventually, after raping the ship and possibly its captain. He could walk back to Union and report events to Capt. Hodges, who was ill-equipped to fight river piracy with a cavalry company, and he could rest assured that everyone would agree that he had done all a man could do. Going north was a sure way to get killed.

He went north.

The going was hard along the riverbank and so Ruff went inland beyond the willows and oaks that lined the Missouri. The moon floated past overhead and he trudged on doggedly, his boots making tiny squishing noises, developing blisters on his feet. He walked and he grew angry. He felt it toward no one in particular, at nothing. He was just angry. Damn them, it was cold and he was tired and he didn't want to walk in squishy boots!

But numbers of people had gotten greedy or ambitious or crazy and they wanted to beat each other at this game they were playing on the river. Justice had been dragged into it. Dragged? Ordered into it by Col. MacEnroe—Ruff put him on the endless list of people, civilizations, events, and customs he was angry with just then—ordered to steer the crazy woman upriver. And paid for the job. Ruff didn't forget that. He was hired on. The army paid him decent wages. They should have. They gambled with his flesh and blood, his life recklessly.

One didn't have to like it. Ruff didn't, and he figured if he ever got his hands on Jack Troll for complicating this mess, he'd rip his gullet out for him.

It grew darker and Ruff took a while to figure out why—his mind was still a little fuzzy at the edges. The moon had dropped beyond the trees, and the stars, huge and brilliant as they were, didn't do much to illuminate the trail ahead.

Ruff was walking through scattered oaks and rolling hills now. The river, to his left, broad and dark, flowed away southward. He paused for breath and searched the wilderness. There wasn't a light anywhere in all the world. Darkness below, starlight overhead. Nothing else.

Where's Troll, then? Ruff asked himself.

Where was Troll and where was the *Jacksonville*? Where, for that matter, was the *River Nymph*? There was just nothing anywhere. Nothing visible. He might have been primeval man alone on the face of a dark, uncaring world. But he wasn't alone—that was illusion—somewhere out there were the river pirates.

And somewhere out there was the greatest Indian army in the history of the continent. It didn't do much to warm a man on a cold and cheerless night.

Ruff Justice walked on. His boots squished, the moon went down, the river flowed past. He found nothing, saw nothing for mile after empty mile.

And then he did.

He had been watching the river for the most part, glancing only occasionally inland. Inland, however, was where he saw the light.

It flickered on, reddish-yellow, and faint, and then flickered off.

Lantern. It had to be a lantern. Ruff stood, hands on hips, staring in that direction. He saw nothing else. There was a lantern, but did that mean it was Jack Troll? It was a long way to go to find out. Perhaps five miles. But there should have been no light there. There were no settlements that Ruff had ever seen or heard rumors of, and at Union they certainly would have known of any new ones. It therefore had to be Troll.

"Inland?" Justice shook his head. It didn't sound right, but his still fuzzy brain finally blundered to the proper conclusion: there was a branch of the river to the east. Troll had his hideout up that waterway.

Ruff started walking. It was a nice night for it, especially in wet boots. So what if his feet were already a mass of blisters. Someone was going to pay for this night. Jack Troll.

It took half of what was left of the night to find the hideout, but find it he did. Ruff lay on the crest of a sandy bluff overlooking the collection of slovenly shacks built up next to the narrow arm of the Missouri.

One of them, the largest, had a palisade built around it like a miniature fort. Jack Troll was many things, but he wasn't crazy. He could hold off anything but a very large army from his river stronghold.

The *Jacksonville* was moored before the little fort.

Men moved along her decks. No one was making an attempt to unload her goods. There was, Troll must have figured, no hurry about that.

Of the *River Nymph* there was no sign.

Had Oakland's people been more alert, or was it simply chance? Had Troll chosen the *Jacksonville* at random and let the other boat go, figuring it was too much to swallow taking on both steamboats?

Or maybe there was someone on the *Jacksonville* who helped things along a little.

A deal with Troll? Why not? There was someone on that boat who had things besides the *Jacksonville*'s best interest—and those of Sally Shore—in mind.

It looked bad below. There were a lot of men, a lot of guns. How the hell did you steal a steamboat back anyway? Ruff was alone, virtually unarmed. He started making his plans.

He wanted first of all to know where the prisoners were. He wouldn't leave the women to Troll and his pirates no matter what.

He watched for more than an hour, measuring, counting heads. He saw no sign of the women, nor of the other prisoners. They could be inside the stockade or on the boat. Either would be difficult to crack.

He started down through the sage and long grass toward the east end of the complex, circling a huge stand of craggy gray boulders that cut gigantic figures against the sky. The moon was down and the going was tricky.

By the time he reached the end of the river camp, he was dripping with perspiration, shivering with the cold of the night. The river was a dark, muddled thing flowing slowly past beneath the big oaks.

The stockade itself was a mile or so west. There were a few buildings scattered about beneath the oaks—warehouses, repair sheds, possibly an armory? That Ruff could have used, but he'd never find it.

Probably inside the stockade, he decided.

He crouched, looking westward and then across the river, seeing a guard walking his slow round, his feet moving heavily as boredom overtook him. If he had been on this side of the river, Justice would have had his try at him. He needed a gun, and needed one badly, although he knew one gun, one man, wasn't going to do the trick here. He was beginning to wish he had gone back to Fort Union.

The man behind him came out of the oak brush before Ruff could turn and draw his boot knife.

"Earl?" the man asked. He came nearer, his head bobbing on the end of a neck that didn't seem to have the strength to support it. It was a moment before Ruff realized why that was. "Wha're doin' here?" the man asked, and Ruff knew—he was dead drunk.

"Sit down," Justice said, and the guard did so, propping his rifle against the tree. Justice took it. The guard nodded and jabbed a finger at Ruff.

"Aren't you cold out here?" the guard asked. "No shirt?" Then he tittered a little, pulling out a large-bowled pipe; he filled it clumsily, spilling half of his tobacco on the ground.

"I went swimming."

"Cold for swimming."

"Very cold. What were you doing?"

"Same shit."

"Where are you posted?" Ruff asked.

The drunk's eyes narrowed with vague suspicion. "You're not Earl."

"No," Ruff agreed.

"Who the hell . . . ?"

"I'm Earl's brother," Justice told him, and the man relaxed a little.

A thought came to his alcohol-fogged mind. "Earl's got red hair. You don't."

"That's right. We had different mothers."

"Earl never told me." He shook his head as if with great sadness. "And I thought we were friends."

"Who's got the jug tonight?" Ruff asked.

"Wiggins." An arm lifted vaguely toward the stockade.

"Big night."

"Sure. All kinda . . . all kinda"—he had broken into a spasm of hiccuping—"goodies on that steamboat."

"The *Jacksonville*?"

"Sure. How many . . . how many . . . how . . ." He succumbed completely to the hiccups for a time.

"Who's watching your post?" Ruff asked, still probing for any usable information.

"Nobody, I don't suppose."

"The back gate?"

"Back gate? We got a back gate now?" the drunk asked. Suspicion had returned. He didn't know this man, but if he was Earl's brother, then he was all right. Besides, there was no one else around for miles but the Sioux. He wasn't one of them . . . was he? The drunk spent some time studying Ruff's face, then he used two fingers to draw a long mustache on his own face. "Ain't Sioux."

"Where were you posted?" Ruff had gained a gun but little else. He was getting tired of trying to pump the man. With the man's hiccups and the slowness of his mind, Justice was getting nowhere fast.

"Smith's barn."

"Over there?" Ruff inclined his head.

"Next to the . . . next to the . . ."

"Next to the stockade, up against the wall?"

"Sure. Got to guard it there. They can get . . . get . . . up and over."

"The Sioux."

"Any damn body. Say, who's got the jug?" the drunk demanded.

"Wiggins."

"Oh, yeah."

"Everyone celebrating pretty hard, are they?" Ruff asked.

"Drunk, some of 'em." The guard scowled disapprovingly. "On duty. Troll'll skin 'em alive."

"Yeah. Where's Troll now?"

"On the boat. The *Jackson . . . Jackson . . . Jackson . . .*"

"You ought to get a drink of water."

"Yeah. Help me up, will ya?"

Ruff helped him up and to the river's edge. When the man stretched himself out to get a drink of water, Ruff tapped him behind the ear with the rifle butt. The drunk hiccuped once and went out. Justice dragged him away from the river so he wouldn't drown—he was going to be in enough trouble for leaving his post.

He had given Ruff some help—whether it was enough or not he didn't know. But he had given him a rifle and the whereabouts of Jack Troll. Troll was on the *Jacksonville*, perhaps counting his loot. Ruff set off downriver, ready to supply Troll with another sort of diversion.

10

You could learn a lot from the Sioux. Ruff Justice had found the floating driftwood tangled in the rushes that grew along the banks of the inlet. With a little work he dragged it free, working in icy, waist-deep stagnant water. Mosquitoes swarmed around his face and shoulders, frogs upriver croaked in a frenzied chorus. The stars beamed down huge and silver.

On board the *Jacksonville* someone was having a little party. Light seeped through several cabin windows, although all of the dark curtains had been pulled. Once, too, someone opened the door to the bathroom and white light spilled out onto the boat's deck before someone shouted angrily and the door was pulled shut again.

It was a celebration of victory, like the Huns or the Goths might have had. Sitting around with captured women, drinking wine, spilling the silver and gold onto the rug before the barbarian leader. Troll's loot wouldn't spill so prettily, but the idea was the same.

The guards walking both decks moved sluggishly. It looked like Wiggins' jug had gotten around pretty well. They didn't even have their heads up; they couldn't have seen an army coming, let alone the single man drifting slowly toward them.

Ruff had his rifle across the tangle-branched floating log, the starlight shone on it, but there wasn't much he could do about that. Otherwise, there wasn't much to see. A long-haired head with angry eyes looking up across the driftwood at the *Jacksonville,* hearing the conversation now, the laughter.

Ruff's teeth ground together. His pulse was strong and cold. He was growing angry, killing-angry.

Anger is a useless emotion, and Ruff knew it, but sometimes it's difficult to keep the bile down, difficult to keep the blood out of your eyes. They had Sally—they couldn't keep her.

Ruff had to kick his legs some to steer the driftwood nearer the *Jacksonville,* and once his foot broke water, but no one heard the small splash.

It was no wonder. As Justice got nearer the boat, the sound from within grew louder, raucous and riotous. Glass was broken, a table turned over, a man bellowed something and then laughed idiotically.

And a woman screamed.

Ruff's eyes went colder yet. The blood in his veins grew hotter.

The driftwood nudged the bow of the *Jacksonville* and Ruff slipped from it to grip the rail and drag himself, dripping water and half-naked, onto the deck of the steamboat.

"Fall in?" A guard was walking hurriedly toward him.

"Yeah. Your turn." Ruff cracked him on the chin with his rifle butt and kicked him overboard. The splash wasn't heard; at least no one rushed toward him. Justice moved on, along the portside cabins, away from the stockade of Trolltown.

The second guard wasn't far along. He emerged from a companionway, his rifle leveled.

"Who're you?"

"Earl," Ruff tried again.

"Earl? What the hell are you . . . ?" He stepped forward, lowering his rifle. He should have kept it up.

Ruff jabbed his own rifle hard into the man's solar plexus, and as the guard folded up, Justice lifted a knee which smashed the river rat's nose and snapped his head back. He sagged to the deck and sat there. Ruff took off the guard's filthy shirt and slipped into it. This one was wearing a belt gun as well, and Justice took that too. The hat was a size too small but Justice put it on. Then with a pair of Winchesters in one hand, the stolen Colt in the other, he started on again.

He found two men crouched beside a dark cabin, drinking whiskey. Ruff stepped in and clubbed one down from behind with his Colt. The other stretched out a hand for his rifle.

"Don't," Justice suggested.

The river rat's hand came away as if that Winchester had been a rattler. "Who're you?" the man asked.

"Where are the prisoners?"

"Boat crew?"

"That's right. Where are they?"

The thug looked around as if hoping help would come. Justice cocked the pistol and the man grew more accommodating.

"In the texas. The men, that is."

"Where are the women?"

"Troll's got 'em." The guard swallowed hard. "One of 'em's aboard. Up front there."

"In the ballroom?" Ruff asked.

"If that's what they call it. The big cabin, up there." His chin indicated the ballroom.

"All right. Get to your feet."

"What for?" Dark, dull eyes glowered at Ruff.

"Because it's a bad night for dying. Get up."

It seemed suddenly like a good idea to the thug and he got up cautiously. Ruff jabbed the Colt down the deck toward the texas.

"That way. You lead off. Don't forget I'm back here with this pistol, will you?"

The river rat didn't answer. He didn't look likely to forget either. They started aft.

There was another guard standing in front of the

texas-deck cabins. This one had a shotgun and looked more alert than those Ruff had encountered to this point. From the corner of his eye Justice could see the ravaged cargo on the deck behind the staterooms. It lay in jumbled confusion, crates ripped open, barrels broken into.

Ruff poked the man in front of him with his Colt, reminding him what he had to lose with a wrong word or move.

"Bailey?" The man with the shotgun was angry. "What in hell are you doing here? You been drinking more? Who's that with you?"

"Earl," Ruff said. He was within a stride of the guard.

"The hell you are . . ." He was a hair too slow bringing the shotgun around. Ruff kicked it from his hands, then kicked him between the legs. The guard went to his knees, folded over, his hands covering his groin.

Ruff tried the cabin door. It was locked. "Where's the key?"

The man on the deck couldn't talk real well. Justice told his other prisoner, "Find that key and keep it quiet. Here—jam this in his mouth." Ruff picked up the guard's own scarf. The river rat looked with hatred at Justice as his friend stuffed the scarf in his mouth.

"Here's the key."

"Good." Ruff motioned to him. "Open the door. Quick."

There was a moment's fumbling and then the door swung open. Ruff Justice stepped into the dark cabin behind the guard. Lydell Cherry was holding a table leg overhead, ready to bring it down on the intruder's skull.

Ruff handed him a rifle. "Use this, it's more efficient."

"Justice!"

"Yeah. There's another man outside the door. Drag

him in and tie them both, gag them properly. We've got to go get the women. Who's in here?"

"Most of us," Cherry answered. Two men brushed by them to drag in the wounded river rat.

" 'S an outrage, 's what it is!"

"The major?" Ruff said.

"Yeah," Cherry said, spitting. "And the green lieutenant." Weeks was too unhappy to resent that. "Cap there, and Wyatt."

"How'd you find us, Justice?" Farley Wyatt asked.

"They've put up signs." Ruff studied Farley, still not able to get a line on who or what he was. But he had been locked up, that meant he wasn't a Troll man. That was all that mattered now. Ruff gave him the other rifle.

"What about me?" Weeks asked.

"There's a scattergun outside."

" 'M in command," Maj. Hawkins said, staggering forward to where Justice and the others held their hurried conference.

"The hell you are," Justice answered sharply.

"He had a flask in his pocket," Cherry explained. "He's been drinking since we were locked up in here."

" 'Tenant Weeks," Hawkins said much too loudly, "you are ordered to give me that weapon and to follow me . . . 's my daughter!"

"It's your daughter," Ruff said, "and if you want her alive, you'll do what I tell you. If not, I'll have you tied and gagged as well. Weeks, if you give him that shotgun, I'll have the same done to you."

"*Loo*-tenant Weeks," the major began with a bellow.

"Tie him," Ruff said.

"You wouldn't dare, scout," Hawkins said, puffing up to twice his normal chest size in his rage.

"Tie him. Weeks?"

The lieutenant shook his head. This wasn't how he had foreseen this trip, how he had seen his military career begin, his relationship with his commanding officer and hopefully his father-in-law. Weeks babbled something and shrugged helplessly.

"It's mutiny," Hawkins had begun to shout.

"I'll do it," Wyatt said. "He can't court-martial me. Andy?" He looked at a young sailor who nodded and helped him, binding Hawkins' wrists behind him, stuffing a cloth in his mouth as he sputtered and went dark in the face.

"If they didn't hear that, it's because they're all drunk abovedecks too," Cherry said.

"Let's hope they are. They're in the ballroom."

Wyatt was finished with his work. "How do we go about it? Storm the place?"

"There's no other way. Try to recapture the boat. Take Troll hostage if we can."

"All right." Farley Wyatt took a deep breath and sighed. They heard him cock his rifle. "Let's have at it."

They went out single-file: Ruff, then Cherry, then Wyatt. The unarmed sailors came next, with Weeks behind covering their tail. A couple of the sailors had picked up tools and lengths of chain. If it came to close-in fighting, some of Troll's people were going to pay a price.

There was only one man guarding the ballroom. Troll must have figured he had plenty of security without extra guards. Ruff tugged down the brim of his borrowed hat, nodded to Cherry, and walked forward to talk to the guard.

"What's going on?" Justice asked. "When are they going to let us have a little fun?"

The guard answered. "The women, you mean? Who the hell are you?"

Ruff walked to the other side of the man with the shotgun, not answering. As the guard turned to follow Ruff with his eyes, Cherry hammered him down from behind. He fell with a muffled thud and Cherry rolled him away. Ruff and his men bunched at the door, hearing the happy confusion within. At a nod from Justice, Cherry kicked the door open and they stepped inside the ballroom, Ruff sliding along the wall to his right, the pistol in his hand elevated and cocked.

One river rat tried for his gun and Ruff shot him, blowing him from his chair. The ballroom fell silent, the pirates frozen in their motion, staring at the doorway with unbelieving expressions.

Ruff walked forward toward the long dining table. It had no cloth on it, little food, but a dozen or so wine bottles, and stuck into the mahogany was a long-bladed knife. Behind the knife surrounded by wine bottles sat Jack Troll, big, red-bearded.

"Who the hell are you?" Troll asked.

Ruff ignored him. Beside Troll sat Sally, her red curls in a tangle, her face smudged, her shirt ripped open. "Move away from him, Sally."

"I said, who the hell are you?" Troll thundered. He put his hands on the table and started to lift himself to his feet. Ruff Justice put a bullet into the table. It shattered a green wine bottle and dug a deep groove in the mahogany. Splinters enough to make Troll's hand look like a porcupine were dug up and embedded in the pirate's fist. Blood trickled onto the table. Smoke drifted between the two men. It seemed that Troll was incapable of feeling pain—or fear. He just sat glaring at Justice, his hand clenching, unclenching.

"Where's the other woman?"

"None of your damn business, boy."

"The next bullet can clip a finger or two, Troll."

"Do it, then, don't talk it!" Troll's face went purple. "Do it. Kill me, if you man enough, boy!"

There was no sense threatening Troll. He was that kind of man—stupid enough to be truly dangerous, truly hard.

"Please, Ruff," Sally said. She had come around the table. She touched his arm. "I know where she is, but we can't help her."

"Where?"

"Inside the stockade. He has fifty men there."

Troll sat there chuckling. "That's right, boy! And if you think you can make me let her go, you full a shit. If you think my men will let her go without my say-so, you're double crazy. They fear what Jack Troll will do to them more than they fear dying, I promise you that."

"Damn you, you bastard!" It was Farley Wyatt who had flared up. They could only watch with astonishment as the kid vaulted the table, scattering glass, slammed his forearm into Troll's face, and knocked him over backward to lie against the floor growling. Farley stuck his rifle muzzle into Troll's face.

"You'll get her out of there."

"Like hell," Troll spat at Farley, and for a second Ruff thought the kid was going to squeeze that trigger.

"Justice," the sailor named Andy called from the doorway. "They must've heard the shot or one of the guards got loose—they're coming from that stockade, must be twenty men."

Justice swallowed a curse. Troll chuckled. "Sally, get us out of here," Ruff said. "Where's Cap? Ed?" The engineer took off at a run. Farley Wyatt grabbed Ruff's shoulder and spun him.

"Where are you going?"

"Getting the hell out. Moving this boat."

"Not without Nancy."

"We've got to go now. Cherry, see if you can collect some guns from these rats, then get up on deck and try to hold them off for a time."

"Not without Nancy," Wyatt shouted again.

"He's not going to let her go, Farley. We can't get to her."

"She goin' be my bride," Troll said. He had risen cumbrously to his feet and was pulling the splinters from his hand with his teeth. "I been wantin' me some sons. I chose that young one for that."

"Ruff!" Sally shouted as the guns opened up on deck.

"Get us moving, Sally."

"Damn you, Justice!" Farley Wyatt was insane with anger.

"Wyatt, I've got Sally to worry about. Everyone on board this boat, the soldiers at Fort Benton who haven't got enough ammunition to hold off Red Cloud, enough clothing and blankets to see them through the winter."

There was a jerk as the *Jacksonville*'s engines started. Farley Wyatt was going crazy. "I'll do it myself. Damn you, I'll do it myself if I have to!"

Ruff looked away and then turned back, swinging a right-hand hook into Farley's jaw. The kid staggered back into the table and went out like a light. Ruff bent, picked up the rifle, and tossed it to Andy.

"Get up on deck. Take these river rats with you—see if they can swim."

Weeks stood staring at Justice, at the unconscious Farley Wyatt, who had blood trickling from his mouth. Jack Troll started laughing again, insanely laughing.

"Get him overboard," Ruff said. He couldn't stand to look at Troll's maniacal face anymore. Weeks didn't have the stomach for handling a man like Troll, so Justice yanked the river pirate to him and then shoved him toward the door. Troll still laughed as he went out on deck, Weeks with a gun behind him.

The gunfire was intense now, but it slowed moments later—presumably the river pirates had recognized their chieftain and didn't want to risk hitting him.

Ruff looked at the unconscious Wyatt, the only person left in the cabin—except for the dead river rat—and then he too went out.

The engines were wide open. Ruff saw a splash as another river pirate was dumped overboard, then Justice shoved Troll over the rail. Rifle fire sang overhead, pinging off the stacks, digging holes in the planking, but the stockade was falling away.

By starlight it seemed very distant, otherworldly. A fortified colony where little tongues of flame licked at the surrounding darkness. The occasional bullet that hit the *Jacksonville* no longer seemed to have any authority. Ruff could see the rats swimming toward the dark shore for a time, but now even they were gone and Cap bleated the whistle once as the steamboat broke free into the big Missouri.

There wasn't much time. Ruff went back to the ballroom. Farley Wyatt was sitting up, holding his head, blood trickling to the floor from his mouth.

"Damn you, Justice," he said.

"Yeah. Get up and let's get going."

"Going where?"

"Why, you ignorant haystacker, you don't think I'm going to leave Nancy Hawkins, do you? Get up, Wyatt. We're going back."

"You and me?"

"You and me." Ruff turned at the sound of approaching boots, knowing who it was. Weeks stood in the doorway in his rumpled uniform listening to the rest of the conversation.

"The way you were talking . . ." Wyatt began.

"I had to talk that way. Did you want Troll to know we were going to have a try at that stockade?"

"No. I guess I wasn't thinking."

"I guess not. You're a pretty impulsive guy, aren't you?"

Wyatt grinned. "I guess so." He was on his feet, rubbing at his jaw. "You pack a punch."

"I suckered you, that's all."

"What do you care about Nancy?" Lt. John Lewis Weeks demanded.

"I care, that's all," Farley said.

"It was more than that. The way you went at Troll . . ." The very idea of bracing a hulking killer like Troll caused Weeks to pale.

"If I'd been in my right mind, I wouldn't have done it," Farley said. "I was just mad, mad clean through, that's all. I've been mad for a long while, I guess."

"You . . ." Slow understanding dawned in Weeks' befuddled mind. "You came aboard this boat just to be with Nancy."

"That's right, soldier," Farley said.

"But how—"

"How? I've been seeing Nancy for most of a year. I had a little place near Fort Armstrong in Iowa. That's where Hawkins was posted last. When I met Nancy, we fell for each other, but her father wouldn't even see me, talk to me, meet me—he was going to have an officer for a son-in-law and not a dirt farmer, and that was it." Farley Wyatt was getting a little heated up now. "Then he and Nancy came west. I came too. Dammit, I'd follow her to Hades. I couldn't catch up with her. By the time I got to Bismarck, she was gone on a steamboat. I bought a horse and headed upriver."

"And when you saw your chance you pulled that charade about the Sioux being after you," Weeks said.

"Sure."

Ruff looked from one man to the other. Their faces were taut masks, their eyes glaring, challenging.

"Why? Why did you follow her?" Weeks asked.

"I'm going to take her away. Take her away and marry her. After seeing her father, I know it's the right thing."

"What if she doesn't want to go?" Weeks asked.

Farley hesitated. "She wants to go. She wants to be with me."

Weeks suddenly understood. "You! It was you in her cabin! It was you she's been sleeping with! It's you that prevents me from having her."

"Easy, Weeks," Ruff said. "Like I told you, the lady's got the right to make a choice."

"She can make her choice. That won't keep me from killing Farley Wyatt."

"Like you wanted to kill *me*," Ruff said sharply. "Dammit, Weeks, haven't you learned anything yet?"

"I said I'd kill him. I will." He spun on his heel then and walked away, his back rigid, his steps heavy and measured.

Farley looked at Ruff. "Are we going to do it?"

"We're going to try. Come one."

Cap was at the wheel, Sally beside him. When Ruff told them what he wanted to do, Sally paled a little but she didn't try to talk him out of it. She knew him better than that.

"What do you want us to do?" Cap MacAdoo asked.

"Very little, Cap. This is an operation for a small party. Me and Farley. Just take the *Jacksonville* in as near to shore as possible. We'll take it from there."

Cap nodded. The steamboat, running with her lights off, eased over toward the eastern bank where a wall of black oaks bulged against the starry sky like low clouds.

"How long before dawn?" Wyatt asked.

"Not long. We don't have the time to make many mistakes." Ruff nodded to Cap MacAdoo. "This'll do it."

Justice turned to Sally, smiled, and kissed her once. He heard her say, "Damn you Ruff Justice," and then he was out on deck, Farley Wyatt behind him, down the companionway to the rail and then over the side, once again into the black, cold Missouri.

11

It was crazy and Ruff Justice knew it, but what else could he do? Leave the Hawkins girl to Troll, that sadistic semihuman? Not if he ever wanted to be able to look at himself in a mirror again.

It had been a long run through the night in wet clothes. Now, with Farley Wyatt lying panting beside him, Ruff looked through the trees at the stockade. Everything appeared to be quiet after a long night of drinking.

"Crazy," Farley Wyatt said, showing that the kid wasn't stupid. "We're crazy."

"See anybody?"

"One guard there, near the dock, another back by the big gate."

Ruff nodded. That checked. That was all he saw, although the trees and the darkness concealed much. The guards had been well-sauced hours ago. The chances were they were still good and drunk, sleeping it off on their posts.

"This way. See that blacksmith's shed?" Ruff whispered. Farley nodded. "Over the wall there."

That was where Ruff's friend from earlier in the evening told him there was access. Hopefully.

Things change in this world. There could have been an army in the woods, a dozen men in the smith's shed. Ruff only hoped that Troll had again been careless enough to allow them to slip into the stronghold.

"They'll never think we'd come back," Farley Wyatt said under his breath.

"I sincerely hope not." Because if Troll did have any such suspicion, a trap would be laid and Ruff was going to walk right into it. "Let's go."

They worked their way through the trees, moving like flitting shadows, Ruff running in a crouch, his eyes alert, his thumb wrapped around the hammer of his Colt. He looked once to the skies, fearing dawn more than anything else at this point. He estimated they still had an hour.

One hour to find a captured woman inside a stockaded town, pull her out from under the noses of fifty armed river pirates, and outrace Troll's men back to the *Jacksonville*, which was moored offshore waiting, her crew armed and ready.

"There it is." Ruff put a hand on Wyatt's shoulder and whispered into his ear, pointing out the smith's shack, which abutted the stockade wall. The two men stood studying the layout: the smith's barn, ten feet high, above it the palings of the stockade like jagged teeth against the starry sky. There were no guards visible on this side of the wall, which ran for fifty feet from the shack to the river. The woods were behind them and to the south, dark, impenetrable to the vision, perhaps alive with guards.

"Let's go," Ruff said. He started forward, Wyatt at his heels.

They reached the shed and found it still unguarded. Sweat dripped from Ruff's forhead. He expected the cries of alarm, the gunshots at any moment. It wasn't real soothing for the nerves.

"Give me your hands," he said to Wyatt.

Farley locked his fingers together and Ruff put a boot in the living stirrup, reaching for the top of the blacksmith's shack as Farley hoisted. Ruff was up and onto the roof with a whisper of sound, the creaking of old planks. He reached down and pulled Farley up to lie beside him on the roof.

They heard nothing but the upriver frogs and crickets. Ruff glanced at Farley, lifted his head, and peered over the palings.

Troll hadn't wasted time building the stockade. It was a slapdash affair, the palings set in holes, lashed with thick rawhide ties. There was also a cross log set four feet from the top where a sentry could walk if he was surefooted. Farther on was a crude ladder tied to the uprights. Below, six or seven shacks shouldered together as if they needed one another for support. Then there was a log house . . .

That one had to be Troll's mansion, the river rat's castle.

Ruff looked at Farley again and stepped over the palings to the log runner. Moving in a crouch, he went swiftly to the ladder and down. Farley was beside him, waiting in the shadows in another minute.

Ruff nearly stepped on a guard.

He was lying drunk or asleep in the shadow of the stockade wall. He rolled over, his eyes going wide with fright and surprise. Ruff clipped him on the temple with the Colt revolver and the man went back to sleep.

They had to move across open ground now to the long building. Farley was grinding his teeth together and Ruff knew what was in his mind. If Troll had touched Nancy . . .

Ruff moved off across the starlit yard. Then he was against the log wall of the building, listening, watching Farley dash toward him. Wyatt slipped on a stone and stumbled. The noise was loud in the night. Ruff had spotted another man sleeping in the open near the shack opposite, but no living, walking guard.

"Sorry," Wyatt hissed. The kid's eyes were as wide as moons. He was shaking with fear, but Farley Wyatt had stuff in him. It would almost be worth all of this if Nancy were to end up with Wyatt instead of the rather flimsy specimen her father had chosen for her.

Ruff nodded and moved to the door. Opening that door was liable to be like lighting a fuse, but there was no backing out now. His boot creaked on the step, the door opened with what seemed a hideous, terrifyingly loud sound. Leather hinges on the door. Split-log door frames. Split-log floor within.

Ruff crept across the floor, eyes darting here and there, searching for—and finding!—Nancy Hawkins.

She was gagged and bound, lying on a thin, straw-filled mat. At the sight of Ruff and Farley her eyes widened, her body's struggling increased violently. The two men moved to her, Ruff's eyes shuttling to the inner connecting door. Beyond that door someone was snoring, snoring like a freight train in a tunnel.

Ruff would have been doing all the people on the river a favor by going through and cutting Troll's throat for him, but there was no telling what kind of booby trap the river rat might have.

They had come to get Nancy, not to kill Troll.

Farley started to remove the gag from Nancy's mouth. Ruff's hand covered his. Ruff pointed to his own lips and mimed silence, making sure Nancy understood. She shook her head vigorously and Ruff took his hand away, letting Farley remove the gag.

The creaking of the floorboards swung Ruff's head around just in time. The man in the doorway was big-shouldered, wearing a plaid coat, carrying a Winchester repeater that spat flame as Ruff rolled to one side, firing from the hip with the Colt.

The guard's rifle bullet dug into the log wall behind Justice; Justice's own .44 bullet lifted the guard to his toes and shoved him backward, spun him half around as the slug ripped its way through his chunky body.

"Come on!" Ruff roared.

Farley half-yanked Nancy to her feet and they ran toward the door as Ruff covered them. The connecting door opened and a massive, naked Jack Troll appeared with a pistol in either hand.

Ruff got off a snap shot that sent Troll ducking back into his room, and then he sprinted for the door himself. A man rushed toward him out of the darkness and Ruff shot his leg out from under him.

Ahead, Ruff could see Farley half-dragging Nancy toward the ladder. Guards, half-asleep, half-drunk, had rushed from their shacks, but they could see nothing. There were no Sioux in the compound, no soldiers. Those alert enough to have done anything had rushed to the gates, where they assumed trouble would begin.

Troll, still naked, appeared at the door of the log house and his voice roared out across the yard. "Stop them! It's the scout. He's got my wife!"

Ruff had reached the ladder and he started up four rungs at a time. Farley had practically thrown Nancy over the palings and onto the roof of the smith's barn. Her skirt had hung up on the pointed tip of one of the logs and ripped partly away. Now Ruff was on the crosspiece that served as a walkway. Rushing toward him fifty feet away was a tall guard with one arm.

The one hand he had was wrapped around a pistol which was turned toward Ruff as a cry came from the guard's mouth. Ruff fired first and the cry became a scream as the guard tumbled from the walkway to the ground below.

"There he is! On the wall! On the wall, damn you!" Troll bellowed.

Ruff shot once in that direction, leapt the wall, and landed on the smith's barn roof. He slid to the ground and caught up with Nancy and Farley Wyatt, who wisely hadn't hung around to wait for Ruff Justice.

"Which way?" Farley panted as Ruff caught up with them.

"East."

"Not north?"

Ruff didn't answer. They were into the trees, the cool dark shadows enveloping them. The sky, seen between the branches of the thick foliage overhead, was beginning to pale. Nancy stumbled once and Ruff grabbed her arm, keeping her up as they ran on.

They stopped for breath a mile on, seeing no pursuit. They've got no horses, Ruff thought, and they're not going to run after us. Not even for Jack Troll.

Or perhaps Troll himself had given it up, realizing that it wasn't worth it, that there would be other boats with new "brides" for him floating down the wide river.

They rose and walked on, circling northward as the sun rose, a great red ball gleaming through the dark, placid oaks, which now were alive with singing birds.

It was midmorning before they sighted the river again and, floating on her in deceptive placidity, the *Jacksonville.*

Farley Wyatt put his hand on Ruff's shoulder. Justice stopped and looked at the dirty, determined face of the kid.

"Oh, no," Wyatt said.

Nancy was hanging onto his arm, her eyebrows drawn together questioningly. Wyatt said it again.

"Oh, no. I'm not going back on that boat. I'm not taking Nancy back to her father. To Weeks. That's it!"

"Farley . . ." Nancy was weary, elated, frightened at once.

"No. Not back into that situation. I know he's your father and you want to do what's right, but that's *not* right. It's just not."

"Farley, we have to," she said. "I couldn't live with you knowing we just ran away."

"We should have just run away a long while ago—that's what caused all of this. Being scared to pick up and do what we wanted to do."

"He's my father!"

"He ought to act like one and concern himself with what's right for you."

"Mister Justice," Nancy said imploringly.

"It's not Justice's business! I'm obliged to him for helping me out, for getting you back for me, but it's not his business what happens now between us."

"Maybe not," Ruff said quietly, "but you're going to have to compromise a little on what you want, Farley."

"What are you talking about?" Wyatt's eyes narrowed a little.

"Just this—keep your shirt on—there's no way out of here. You've got no horses. If you did, you'd have a lot of Indian territory to cover. You can't go back down the river even if you had a way. Troll is still there. That only leaves one way. Upriver on the *Jacksonville.*"

"Never!"

"Farley, he's right," Nancy said, turning him, holding both of his shoulders as she looked up with those intent amber eyes. "There's just no other choice. I'd go with you anywhere, but there's *nowhere to go.*"

It was a long while before he answered. "All right!" he said at last, banging his fist against his thigh. "All right, all right! If you both think it has to be, then it has to be." He took a deep breath through his mouth. "We'll go on down—they must be tired of waiting for us."

Cap had the engines cranked up before they had waded to the *Jacksonville.* Weeks and Maj. Hawkins, looking somewhat sober, helped them up over the rail. Sally stood by, hands on hips.

"Well," she said, "think you've held us up long

enough? The *River Nymph* is probably a hundred miles upriver by now."

"Get us going," Ruff said, "and quit talking about it." He swung a leg up over the rail and sat there dripping water on the deck. "You're not fooling anyone with that tough talk anyway, Sally Shore."

She grinned then and went to him, hugging him for a minute. "Get it going, Cap!" She moved her arm in a cranking motion and the big paddle wheel started turning and they were off again, after Griff Oakland and his *River Nymph*.

12

They began to find white water. The creeks, swollen with the upcountry rain, rushed out of the surrounding hills and joined the already quickly flowing Missouri. The river ran broad and gray-green, blanketed here and there in the shallows with white water.

Northward the skies had begun to gray and cloud, and it looked like the rain that had been holding back was ready to sweep southward.

"Bad stretch, Justice!" Sally had to shout above the roar and hiss of the river. The *Jacksonville,* never meant for this kind of water, bucked and rolled awkwardly.

"You'd better get used to it," Ruff told her. The wind blew his long hair back from his face. The fringes on his buckskins flapped in the breeze. "There's a long stretch of this to come. The river's narrowed by the rocky cliffs. The water's got to go somewhere and so it wriggles and curls and rises."

"We'll make it," she yelled. "We'll make it through."

"Sure," Justice said, but Sally didn't hear him. She was looking straight ahead, upriver, hoping to catch sight of the *River Nymph,* perhaps hoping to see it foundering. She was going on on hope and courage. Ruff hadn't told her the whole truth.

He had said there was a long stretch of water like this to get through, miles of it. The truth was that this was as smooth as a washbasin compared to the stuff farther along.

Nancy Hawkins was at the rail holding on as if for dear life when Ruff went aft. Her face was pale, washed out—it wasn't all from motion sickness.

"Oh, hello, Ruff."

"A cheerful howdy," he jibed.

"Who's cheerful?"

"Where's Farley? He ought to be able to cheer you up some."

"That's just it. We've decided to be logical and mature about this and not confront Father until we've reached Fort Benton. Is there an army chaplain there, Mister Justice?"

"I believe so."

"Because we need to get married . . . in the worst way."

"I know." He recalled Farley asking him what sort of facilities there were at Fort Union, realizing only later that Farley wanted to get married and take a stage east with Nancy.

"It's hard waiting . . ." Her voice dipped and rose as the *Jacksonville*'s bow lifted and then came down with a racketing splash that sent sheets of water ten feet high out from either side. "Is Sally Shore crazy? Is the army?" She paused and smiled. "Or is it just me?"

"All of us a little," Ruff answered. "Let's say that beating the *River Nymph* to Benton probably means as much to Sally just now as marrying Farley does to you."

Nancy shook her head at that implausible fact. Her chestnut ringlets bounced breezily as she did that. She looked small and very charming. A moment later she was at the rail looking very sick.

Ruff wasn't far from it himself. Holding on to the rail attached to the cabin deck, he walked aft. He was looking for Weeks or Farley or both, wanting to find out how things stood between them, not wanting Nancy to be a widow before she was a bride.

He found Lydell Cherry first. The mate was in a violent mood. "Was it you, Justice? I thought you were straight—maybe I was wrong."

"Maybe so. What are you talking about?"

"Somebody cut our anchors loose."

"They what?"

"Cut the lines on the bow and stern anchors both and overboarded them. You know what that means?"

"Yes, I do," Ruff said.

Cherry went on as if he hadn't answered him. "We can't keep ourselves from being pushed downstream if the engines falter. At night we're going to have to moor to something ashore." He waved a hand toward the gray stony bluffs. "If we can find anything ashore to moor to. I've got to report it to Sally." Cherry looked skyward. "She'll hit the ceiling."

"Was it you, Cherry?" Ruff asked.

"Me! How in hell could you ask that?"

"Because I know it wasn't me and I can't figure out who else it might have been."

"It wasn't me, and if I find out who it was, I'll strangle 'em. Sally deserves a little good luck. Hell, maybe it was your friend Wyatt and his little woman wanting to float back down to Lincoln like two love-bugs on a leaf."

"I doubt that," Ruff said, "but there's obviously someone on board who wants us to fail."

"Like you?"

"Me? What do I care, Cherry? I'm on this job for wages."

"Yeah, and maybe Griff Oakland offers better wages than Sally."

"Maybe so, but I wouldn't know. I never saw Griff Oakland until we hit Mandan. You boys, you all knew each other back down the river—that's what Sally told me."

"Know him, that don't mean we like him."

"If the wages are good enough, maybe you don't have to like the boss, Cherry."

"You bastard, I ought to smash your teeth in." Cherry took a step forward and then had to grip the walking rail as the *Jacksonville* lifted off the water again. Spume washed across the deck and Cherry's enthusiasm for fighting seemed to wash away with it. "I've got to tell Sally and Cap. I don't know how we're going to tie up tonight."

He went by and Ruff let him go. He believed Lydell Cherry, believed the first mate was not the turncoat—the man had too much loyalty to Sally Shore.

Who, then? The answer still wouldn't come. Ruff went aft. He was in time to stop the duel, but just barely.

The two young men faced each other across the texas deck, pistols in their hands. Three crew members, unbelieving, stood by doing nothing. Weeks was to Ruff's left, the closer of the two. As their arms went up, Justice launched himself across the unsteady deck to shoulder Weeks to the planks.

"Damn you, damn you!" Weeks' gun had clattered free and now he lay cursing and writhing, trying to get Ruff Justice off him. It did no good. Ruff wasn't moving.

"Let him up," Farley was shouting. "He needs it."

Instead, Ruff clipped the young officer on the chin and rose to stand glaring at the sailors around him. "You men going to let them kill each other? Andy?"

"It was their fight, Mister Justice."

"It was your problem. This is your boat. Take this one"—he pointed at Weeks—"and lock him up in a cabin. And take the gun from Mister Wyatt's hand."

"Justice," Wyatt protested, "it wasn't my doing."

"Get that gun, Andy, and if you see him with another, lock him up as well."

"I guess we ought to check with Mister Cherry or Captain Shore," Andy objected.

"I'll tell Captain Shore what I've done, don't you worry about that. Just get that soldier out of here and locked up."

The boat rolled again just then and everyone grabbed for balance, but when the *Jacksonville* was running flat once more, Weeks was taken away and Farley Wyatt handed over his gun.

"It really wasn't my doing, Mister Justice," Wyatt said. "He came hunting me. I couldn't back down. And he'll be back. You know that as well as I do. You might as well have let me finish it now. He'll be back and he won't be satisfied until it's done, one way or the other."

The *Jacksonville*'s whistle blasted three times and then three more, excited, short whistles, and Ruff craned his neck forward to have a look.

"They've caught her, damn them," he said with a kind of pride. "They've caught the *River Nymph.*"

Not quite, but at least Oakland's boat was visible now. The side-wheeler was making tough work out of negotiating the white water. If anything she was having a harder time than the *Jacksonville,* which seemed to be barely creeping along, swaying and rolling, threatening to switch ends. When Ruff reached the wheelhouse, Sally Shore was ecstatic.

"We'll beat the bastard yet," she shouted, waving a fist. Cap's face was red with concentration or exhilaration, Ruff couldn't tell which.

"That's it," Cap said, "run it into those rocks, you damn fool."

Cherry was there was as well, scowling, silent, his hand on the whistle cord.

Justice told Sally what he had done with Weeks and Farley.

She only nodded her head. "All right, if you had to." Her attention was on the *River Nymph,* however, only on the *Nymph.* "Move over, Cap," she said, taking the wheel. "I want to be piloting her when we pass him."

Cap stepped aside as Sally positioned herself behind the big brass-mounted wooden wheel, and one hand on the whistle cord, she steered the sternwheeler upriver in pursuit of her rival.

An hour later they were in deep shadow cast by the stony cliffs, but the *River Nymph,* which had steadily been falling back in the heavy current, was fifty feet ahead. They could see sailors on her deck now, and in another few minutes they saw big Griff Oakland shaking his fist at Sally Shore as the *Jacksonville* steamed past, her whistle piping gleefully.

"Now," Cap said at length, "we can start to worry."

"To worry?" Ruff's forehead furrowed. "We've got the lead back."

"We'll never keep it overnight," Cherry explained. "No anchors, remember? If we cut off the engines, we'll drift back. It'll be dark in an hour. See if you can find us a place to tie up; I sure as hell can't. No trees, nothing to tie to."

"And we can't steam on at night," Cap pointed out. "Not in this kind of water."

"You two worry enough," Sally said. "We'll probably find calm water before night, right, Ruff?"

"Not in this stretch of river!" They all held on as the *Jacksonville* hit a shelf of curling water and dropped her bow ten feet, slapping down hard before she righted as Sally Shore fought the wheel.

"Then we'll find a way to moor up. Damn, saddled with a bunch of old ladies," Sally said, clamping her jaw shut. The worry showed through the armor of gruffness.

Cap shrugged at Justice and went to the front of the wheelhouse to peer at the foaming river, the stony banks as the sunlight dimmed and faded, the shadows creeping out to make a dark, savage creature of the river.

A pyramid-shaped wedge of rock jutted up through

the white water. In midriver it posed a treacherous threat to the steamboat. If it had been ten minutes later, the *Jacksonville* might have gutted herself on the knife edge of the stone slab, but Sally saw it and started to take her boat to port.

"That!" Ruff Justice said suddenly, gripping Sally's shoulder so tightly that she flinched.

"What are you talking about, Ruff? Let go now, I've got to veer away from that rock."

"Veer away, hell! Get straight on to it, Sally, that's your anchor."

"Are you crazy?" Cherry asked with disgust.

"Maybe. You've been asking for something to moor to. What's wrong with that rock? It's not going anywhere. It's in the middle of the river, safe from Indians."

"It can't be done," Cherry said.

"Sure it can," Ruff insisted. "Sally?"

"Cut back the engines," she told Cap.

"Sally, if you mess this up . . ."

"Shut up and I won't. Ruff's right, if we ease up to it . . . Get a bowline ready, Cherry. Make it two, and make 'em stout!" she said across her shoulder.

"I can't ask a man to try tying up to that while you hold against the current."

"Then do it yourself, Lydell," Sally shouted angrily. It was growing rapidly dark. There wasn't much time to argue. With a growl Cherry started down to the lower deck, Ruff at his heels.

"What the hell are you doing here?" Cherry demanded.

"I'm going over. I'll take the line if you're not up to it."

"Who said I'm not up to it?"

"I don't want to argue. Get us those lines, Cherry!"

The *Jacksonville* was fighting the bucking current; water frothed over the deck. The rock, huge and dark, like a river beast's giant horn waiting to gut the *Jacksonville*, was only a few yards off. Sally feathered the throttles, coming in closer as the current tried to rip the steamboat away from its objective and hurl it back downstream. The engines stammered and groaned as their speed was cut to stalling point.

Cherry was back with Andy and two heavy lines the thickness of Ruff's wrists. "Tie it off, tie it off," Cherry shouted above the water's roar. The *Jacksonville* slewed sideways violently and Andy had his feet knocked out from under him. Rising, cursing, he tied the first line to a huge cleat on the foredeck. Justice was stripping off his shirt.

"I said I'd do it," Cherry panted, shoving Ruff aside. It was nearly too dark to see the mate's face, but Ruff could feel the heat of anger rising from his body. Justice laughed out loud.

"Now I've got it," he said. "It's Sally Shore—you're in love with her."

Cherry was dead silent for a long minute as he stood with the heavy line coiled around his shoulder. "Go to hell, Ruff Justice," he said finally, and then he was to the bow, stepping over the rail, poised as the *Jacksonville* surged toward the rock and then was pushed away. If Cherry missed, he ran the risk of being crushed between the boat and the rock, of being carried away downriver.

He missed.

Cherry's foot landed on the stone as he leapt across the ribbon of foaming water separating the boat from his goal, but he slid away, going down hard, his face banging against the rock. The river sucked him under.

"Back it off!" Ruff Justice yelled, but Cherry was already gone. He turned to Andy. "Bring a line aft, move it, dammit!"

Then Ruff was running the length of the deck on the port side, peering into the dark water. Reaching the texas deck, he saw the head bobbing past, saw an arm reach out feebly, and Justice launched himself into the water.

It was biting cold, swirling, shoving at him, threatening to suck him down. Ruff surfaced, shook the hair from his eyes, and spotted his objective: the stunned, drifting first mate of the *Jacksonville.*

He swam toward him, fighting the current, using it. Twice he touched Cherry's collar before he got a grip on it, his fingers wrapping themselves in the fabric of his shirt. It was cold, very cold, and it was dark. Ruff could see nothing. He only knew he had to get upriver and so he started swimming, trying to move against the rapid flow of the river.

It loomed up huge and black against the sky: the *Jacksonville* had backed to meet them. Its big stern wheel was only ten feet from Ruff's head and he stroked frantically away from it, towing Cherry, not knowing if the mate was alive or dead. He found the line almost by accident. His hand struck something that did not belong in the liquid coldness and then the voice, impossibly distant cried out.

"The line. Grab the line, Mister Justice!"

It slipped out of his grasp like an eel. Ruff grabbed for it again, frantically. The river was trying to tug Cherry from his grasp, but Justice wouldn't let him go. Ruff went under, choking on a mouthful of water. When he came up again, the rope was there and he clutched at it, locking it in his grip. It pulled through his hand as the line went taut, but a huge knot near the end of the rope snugged against his clenched fist and Ruff was towed toward the steamboat, which rocked and panted in the water, trying to hold her precarious position.

"Right here. I've got you."

Arms reached down and yanked Justice up. He still held Cherry's collar and now he felt the weight on his arm relieved as they hauled the mate aboard. Someone had a lantern and they bent over Cherry as Ruff coughed up a gallon or two of Missouri River water.

"Are you all right, Mister Justice?"

"How's Cherry?"

"Bad gash on his head. Stunned more than anything, I'd guess. How about you?"

"Get me up," Ruff answered, and they lifted him to his feet.

"You'd better take it easy, Mister Justice."

"Sure." He was already walking forward, shaking his head to try to clear the water from his ears. Sally was at the bow looking helplessly at the dark river, the black tongue of rock. The heavy line was in her hand. Ruff took it from her.

She turned, startled. "Oh, Ruffin! God, I thought . . . I didn't dare go back. I didn't want to know. How's Cherry?"

"He's all right. The man's in love with you, you know."

"He's what? What are you doing with the line?"

"What do you think? It's still got to be done, doesn't it?" He hung the coil of rope over his neck and under his arm. "Hell," he said, grinning, "I'm already wet. Get up in that wheelhouse. Nudge this steamboat up to that rock. I'll make like it's a front porch and just step on over."

"Like Cherry did!"

"Cherry was unlucky."

Sally, who thought that Cherry was very lucky—to be alive—went away shaking her head. Ruff Justice would have his way. Besides, there was really no other choice. They couldn't steam on in the darkness, would drift backward. She snarled at Cap when she entered the wheelhouse.

"Damn fool's got more nerve than a madman." Or maybe he was a madman. She could just make out Ruff swinging his legs over the rail, watching and waiting as the *Jacksonville* plunged toward the jagged, jutting rock again.

The boat surged forward and then was pushed back by the relentless river. Ruff stood poised, measuring the distance, timing his leap, eyes straining against the darkness, water misting into his face.

The *Jacksonville* slid backward and then started toward the rock once more. Ruff jumped for it. His foot struck, slipped away, and he clawed out frantically with his hands. The current tugged at his heels, threatening to draw him away as it had Cherry, to send him down the long stony chute of the river.

He found a grip. It wasn't much, but his torn hand found enough of a fingerhold to keep him on the rock while he planted his feet and caught his breath. The water, to midthigh, was freezing, the current more powerful than ever.

He started to climb. He reached the pinnacle of the anchor stone in seconds, but finding a place to tie the line was more difficult. He decided finally he was going to have to loop the entire rock, and he found himself wishing Cherry had made it—his knots would be surer.

Justice built a big loop and, using a running bowline, cinched down the huge rope as well as he could. It would have to do. There would be no more chances.

He stood atop the rock, and as the *Jacksonville* surged forward again, he coiled the remaining rope and tossed it to Andy on the steamboat's deck. Andy secured it and Ruff stood waiting, shivering, holding his breath. Would it work?

Slowly the *Jacksonville* backed from him, the line going taut, rising from the black water. Then the paddle wheel was disengaged and the steamboat lay dead in the water, yanking at its tether like an angry dog. It held.

The rope held; with luck it would hold through the night. Ruff shook his head. It was something he didn't want to try again. He had been lucky, so had Cherry. It was a wonder neither was drowned, cut to pieces by the paddle wheel or swept away downriver to be pounded against the rocks, broken on them.

Ruff slipped down the rock, got a grip on the

anchor line, and started hand-over-handing it toward the *Jacksonville,* the angry dark river still pulling at him, snapping at his heels.

Hands helped him up and he stood shivering on the deck. Sally hugged him and said, "God, tall man, what would I do without you?"

"How's Cherry?"

"I haven't seen him yet."

"Let me dry off and let's do that."

She looked at him oddly and then withdrew a little—physically and emotionally withdrew. "Ed, you or one of your people will have to stand by in the engine room. If we lose that line, we'll need to start up immediately. Cap or Andy or me will be up top . . ."

Ruff let the river sounds drift her words away as he walked to his cabin, stripped off his clothes, and dried off. He sat on the bed for a minute, exhausted, chilled to the bone. The door opened and he looked up to see Sally standing there.

"I'll be right with you," Justice said. He rose, crossed the cabin naked, and stepped into his dry pants.

"What you said about Cherry," Sally asked, "was it true?"

"About him loving you? Yes. Probably from way back, but Jolly won you. He doesn't like me hanging round you."

"The old hard-shell," Sally said. She stood with her arms crossed beneath her breasts, leaning against the door, her eyes distant. Ruff finished dressing and brushed his hair quickly. "The old bastard," she repeated at intervals in wonder.

"Let's go see how the old bastard is," Ruff said.

He took her arm and started out on deck. The boat was rocking violently but the line seemed to be holding fast. They found Cherry, his head bandaged, sitting up in bed.

"Thought you'd deserted, Lydell," Sally said, sitting on his bed.

Cherry frowned and looked at Ruff. "Thanks, Justice. They told me it was you."

"That's all right."

"I don't like you, though. Never will."

"That's all right too," Ruff replied.

They sat with the mate for a while until weariness closed his eyes; then they left him, blowing out the lamp, stepping out quietly, shutting the cabin door.

"There you are, skipper!" It was Andy, looking excited and a little pale. He rushed toward them across the rolling deck.

"What is it, Andy?"

"Well . . ." He looked at Ruff and then at Sally again. "It's Major Hawkins, skipper. He's dead."

13

He was dead, all right.

Maj. Hawkins lay sprawled against his cabin floor, one arm outstretched as if he were reaching for something, one leg bent under him. Blood made a dark sticky pool beneath his head. One of his pointed, waxed mustache tips was frayed into something resembling an unraveling rope end. He was definitely dead.

When Ruff and Sally reached the cabin, Nancy Hawkins was sitting up in a wooden chair, her nose red, her eyes swollen. In her hand was a crumpled handkerchief. She moved her lips as Ruff entered, but said nothing audible.

Farley Wyatt stood behind her, his hand on her shoulder. The kid looked sad, but his sorrow must have been more for Nancy than for the army officer he hated.

"What happened?" Sally asked.

"He died," Nancy said limply.

"How?"

Both of the younger people shook their heads. Ruff crouched down beside the body, lifted it enough to see the broken whiskey bottle beneath it, and let it sag back. Beside the body was a low cabinet, and on the corner of the cabinet blood and hair.

"What do you think, Ruff?"

"I *think* he was drunk on a rocking, pitching boat, lost his balance, and struck his head on the cabinet."

"He wasn't drunk," Nancy insisted.

Ruff looked at her defiant amber eyes. If Hawkins hadn't been drunk, it would have been the first time in days. He didn't want to argue with the girl—she had apparently loved her father no matter what he was.

"All right. He simply fell," Ruff said.

"He wasn't murdered?" Sally asked bluntly.

Nancy stiffened. Farley Wyatt squeezed her shoulder violently and leaned forward, his upper lip twitching at the corner.

Ruff sighed inwardly. He had considered murder too, but it hadn't seemed like a good idea to mention it in front of the victim's daughter and the prime suspect, which was what Farley Wyatt would have to be considered.

"I don't think so," Ruff said. Honestly he didn't know. He rose and dusted his hands off, although there was nothing on them.

"What do you want to do with the body?" Sally asked. She was excessively blunt and just barely polite, but Ruff recognized this manner in her. Sally Shore tended to get blunt when she was frightened or nervous. She was both now.

"I . . . I don't know what to do." Nancy looked at Farley, who didn't know what to do either.

"We can bury him in the water," Sally said. "He'll never make it to Fort Benton, not in any fit condition . . ." Even Sally Shore realized she was getting a little too forthright.

"Ruff?" Nancy asked.

"Want me to take care of things?"

"Please. Do what needs to be done. I can't think."

Ruff nodded. Turning to Andy, he said, "Get a couple of sailors in here. We'll take him out."

Ruff stepped to Nancy, touched her cheek, and

smiled. Then he turned and went out onto the slanting, moving deck.

Sally was there beside him. "Well?" she asked.

"Have you got a length of chain "

"Of course."

Ruff looked at the dark, swirling water. "Wrap him in it. Send him home."

Justice was silent, leaning over the rail. Sally Shore realized suddenly that she was seeing something else, a different part of Ruff Justice. A silent, thoughtful man aware of his own mortality, a man who dealt with death constantly and yet hated it. Feared it! Who didn't? But one never had that impression with Justice. The way he lived—spitting in the face of death, challenging it—why, it was almost as if he wanted to die. But that was absurd. Why would a man like Justice, who had so much, want to die?

"He wasn't much of a man," Ruff said finally. "But maybe he was once. Maybe life was just too big a disappointment."

Then he turned and walked away toward his cabin, leaving Sally Shore to wonder if life wasn't a disappointment to Ruff Justice as well, if life wasn't something that had to be prodded awake, to the very edge of recklessness, to be savored.

"Take him forward and find a length of chain," Sally said to the sailors who walked past her with the body of Maj. Hawkins. Then she went forward as well, cursing the night and death and male creatures.

At dawn the line still held. Two strands had frayed through, but the *Jacksonville* had spent a safe if uncomfortable night. The engines were started, the line cut free, and the big steamboat started on.

Sunrise painted the stony walls of the canyon deep red and shifting purple. Ruff Justice watched it all in silence. He was, he decided, weary of the boat and the river. He wished for a good horse under him, a small campfire on the empty, broad land, nothing else.

But the river was unending.

They emerged from the canyon at last and the river was wider once more, the current slower. Trees began to appear along the shore again. Oak and cottonwood, spruce and pine. The land was rolling hills, ripe with green grass. The rainstorm that had been threatening seemed to have withdrawn; the sky was deep blue, clear with only a few white puffy clouds scudding southward to paint racing shadows against the grassland.

"Sioux."

Cherry, his head wrapped in a bandage, pointed toward the southern shore. Two or three miles distant they saw them. Sioux they were, but not a handful of renegades. A nation was on the move: Warriors on horseback, other horses pulling travois; women walking, carrying children; dogs running alongside in packs. Hundreds upon hundreds of them.

"Some of Red Cloud's people."

Cherry bit at his lip tensely. "They'll see us. Think they'll come after us?"

Ruff shrugged. Whatever he said would be a guess. "I don't think so, no. I think they've got more important things on their mind. Survival. War. A big war."

The steamboat would be a nuisance or a novelty depending on how they looked at it, or so Ruff thought.

"But if they knew we had goods for Fort Benton—ammunition and guns . . . ?"

Ruff didn't answer. He didn't have to. If Red Cloud knew that this steamboat was a war canoe, then he would destroy it. There were no ifs about that. He had Benton encircled and he meant to close it down, to burn it to the ground as he had Fort Peck. If he had to destroy the *Jacksonville* first, he would.

"Those Indians," Justice said, "don't look to be on the warpath. They've got warriors with them, but there's too many women, too many kids. I don't think they want our blood or our goods. You keep watching, Cherry. You just keep watching. When you see a band of Sioux, warriors only, and they're wearing bonnets, their horses' tails tied, their faces painted—well, you let me know then and we can all spend some time trying to remember how to pray."

It wasn't really comforting. The Sioux continued to ride and walk past, unconcerned apparently with the boat. Sally had her men on deck, armed, watching.

"Just so none of them gets trigger-happy," Ruff said. "Squeezing a trigger now is the same as signing a death warrant for everyone on board."

By midday there were no more Sioux to be seen, but everyone on the *Jacksonville* had been sobered by the sight. They were deep in hostile territory now, and those who had thought getting through the rapids was half the game began having second thoughts.

There was a reason, after all, that those supply wagons hadn't been able to get through to Fort Benton.

They had to have wood again, and although nobody was thrilled with the idea, they went ashore when they found a stand of age-grayed oaks. Ruff was among the six men who stood guard with rifles from the top of the wheelhouse. The breeze was cool, the clouds drifting south again. The work party seemed to be having little trouble.

At the sound of the toot their heads turned southward again. They could hardly believe their eyes. It was Oakland. The bastard, give him credit, was catching up once more, the twin stacks of the *Nymph* blowing white smoke into the changing sky.

"Can hardly believe it," Cherry said in something approaching admiration. "The son of a bitch is with us."

"Can he beat us to Fort Benton?" Ruff asked.

"Hell, anything can happen. I would've said no, but that side-wheeler seems to be taking to this river.

Tom McCulloch's his chief engineer, and Tom's a whiz . . . Maybe, just maybe." He hollered at the top of his lungs, "Damn you men, get that wood cut! Get on back, we're leaving! If you're coming, come along now!"

They came, all right; no one thought Lydell Cherry was a bluffer. They knew the big first mate too well. They rowed the dinghy frantically toward the *Jacksonville* as Ruff and the other guards slid from the wheelhouse roof to the deck. The *River Nymph* was coming on fast now, and as the *Jacksonville*'s engines roared to life, they could see that Oakland was going to overtake them.

"How?" Cherry asked in amazement. "He can't have run at night. He's got to to stop for fuel too!"

Already they could see the answer. Oakland wasn't stopping for fuel or anything else.

"The bastard's torn half his texas deck up!"

He had at that. Gambling all on the army contract, which would mean years of work for many boats, Griff Oakland had started cannibalizing his boat, feeding wood from the cabins and upper decks into his fireboxes.

The *River Nymph* wasn't stopping for wood, for anything.

She churned past the *Jacksonville*, her twin wheels throwing up bright fans of water as the *Jacksonville*'s crew stood hurling futile invective after her.

Sally Shore was storming.

"Open those throttles, Cap! What is this, a Fourth of July picnic cruise? Where's Ed? Hasn't he got anyone who can make those engines turn right. What's that stammering in number one? More fuel, boys! I want that wood below and I want to see those fireboxes glowing!"

But the *Nymph* was pulling away steadily and there was nothing Sally could do about it immediately. Benton was a long way off yet, but was it far enough away to overtake the *Nymph*?

"Who makes the decision now?" Cherry asked Justice. "I mean, you're army. Who makes the decision on the contract? Major Hawkins was supposed to."

"I don't know. The old commander at Benton, I guess."

"You don't know him?"

"Haven't been this way for a year. I have no idea who it is," Ruff answered.

"He'll have to give it to Sally. He'll have to know Oakland's a thief and a pirate."

"How's he going to know that, Cherry?"

"I'll tell him, by God!" Cherry was hunched forward, his fists clenched, the bandage on his head stained with blood. "I'll tell him! Sally has to win this contract. She has to. You tell me, Justice, what's she going to do without a boat? And she loses the *Jacksonville* without a contract with the army."

"I know," Ruff said, but as he watched the *Nymph* steam on, apparently by far the faster boat, the chances of Sally Shore winning seemed slim.

A minute later they seemed a hell of a lot slimmer.

The number-one engine had been stuttering and knocking, and now there was an explosion below and the boat was rocked violently. Fire spewed out of the engine room. Justice and Cherry looked at each other and took off on the run.

Below, they were fighting the flames with buckets of sand. Ed, his arm and face already burned, was trying to slap some of the fire out. Justice hauled the engineer out of there struggling.

"I gotta put it out," he shouted.

"They're getting it. You can't put it out with your body."

Sally was there suddenly, and Cap. People were shouting conflicting instructions as the flames continued to gout from the engine.

It took half an hour to put it out. When they were through, they were left with one engine and a blackened engine room. There was a gaping hole in the ceiling and one wall had been destroyed. Ed, the engineer, was badly burned and one of the fire fighters had suffered from smoke inhalation.

"Lucky, anyway," Ruff Justice said. His face was smudged, his hand bleeding.

"Lucky!" Sally looked at him with blank eyes. "How can you say that, Ruff?"

"The whole boat could've gone down. More people might have been seriously hurt."

"The boat might as well have gone down," she snapped. "What's the difference if she stays afloat? She's never going to beat Oakland's boat to Fort Benton on one engine. She may as well have gone down; I'll lose her anyway."

"Don't give up. Oakland can't have all the luck."

"Luck! This isn't luck, Justice; it's sabotage, and you know it."

Ruff looked around. Yes, he guessed it was. Ed would have to tell them exactly what had been done to the boiler, but it was sabotage. Sally's enemy was still aboard the *Jacksonville*.

Sally lifted her hand and waved it feebly. Then she slapped her thigh and ordered, "Hell! Get the other engine going. Maybe Oakland will run aground. Maybe the Sioux will get him. Let's give it a try."

"Plucky lady," Farley Wyatt said.

"She is that," Ruff agreed.

The engine roared to life and they went out on deck through the burned timbers and ashes.

"How's Nancy doing?"

"As well as you could expect. It hasn't been a hell of a lot of fun."

"No." Ruff was looking to the wheelhouse, his mind weighing something he didn't enjoy thinking of.

"What's the matter, Justice? Still think I killed the major?" Farley smiled. "It was written all over your face."

"No, I don't think so now, Farley."

"It was an accident, then."

"No. No, it was no accident. Excuse me, Farley, will you? I've got some serious thinking to do."

"Sure." Puzzled, Wyatt stepped back and let Ruff go by. Then he settled at the rail, feet crossed, to watch the silver-blue Missouri widen and begin its last great western turn before it ran past Fort Benton.

Ruff found Lt. John Lewis Weeks in his cabin. The guard outside the door said he hadn't even made a sound except for one long, pained groan.

"How you doing, Weeks?" Ruff said.

The young cavalry officer looked up and shook his head. He seemed to have lost a lot of weight in the past few days. His cheeks were scooped out. There were dark smudges around his eyes.

"Not good. Sick, Justice. Sick all through. I've been doing some serious thinking down here."

"Have you? Come to any conclusions?"

"Yes. I've decided I'm the damnedest fool that ever wore army blue. I'd like to apologize to you and then to Wyatt and Nancy, and then walk right out of their lives."

"Did they tell you the major was dead?"

"That what?" Weeks looked up in pure shock, his eyes bulging, his already pale face going sheet-white. "Why would you say a thing like that?"

"Because it's true."

"What happened?"

"Murder, I think."

"And you think I—"

Ruff shook his head. "No, I don't. I can't see you murdering Hawkins. But I think I know who did it."

"Who?" Weeks' face grew dark with slow anger.

Justice cautioned him. "You take it easy. Your temper'll get you in trouble again. It's not going to help you become a good officer either."

"I'm starting to think I don't have what it takes to be a good officer at all."

"You have it. You just start looking for it. Start looking for the man you're carrying around inside of that boy's body."

Weeks didn't like that characterization, but it seemed to strike home. He shook his head slowly. "What was all the excitement—the explosion?"

"One of the engines blew up."

"Blew up!"

"It was tampered with."

"Who would do that?"

"The murderer. Want to come along and help me nail him?"

14

Lydell Cherry still had his head bandaged. He looked around, scowling, as Ruff and Weeks entered the wheelhouse, where Sally and Cap urged the crippled *Jacksonville* after the far distant *River Nymph*.

"What're you doing with the soldier boy, Justice?" Cherry asked. His dark eyes were brooding, clouded.

"I just wanted to bring him along. It's time we let him out of his cabin, I guess, and locked up the man who's been sabotaging the boat, the man who killed Major Hawkins . . . isn't that right, Cap?"

"If you mean me," Cherry exploded, "I'll—"

"I don't mean you, Cherry. You're guilty of nothing but hardheadedness and of loving Sally Shore. I mean Cap MacAdoo."

"You're wrong," Sally said. "It's ridiculous! Cap has been with me since—"

"Since the *Birmingham* went down, I know. Since the *Birmingham* with Joe Jolly at the wheel went down."

Cap smiled around his pipe. His white-whiskered face glowed at the cheeks. His eyes sparkled.

Justice stepped to him. "You drink, do you, Cap? That whiskey smell stays with a man, you know. Get a little splashed on your coat?"

"You're crazy," Sally said.

"Sure. Figure it out. Figure out who had an opportunity to do everything that's happened. Who had the run of the ship, who could get into the engine room now after one attmept at sabotage, with all the crew watching, and not be suspected? It wasn't Cherry who killed the major. He was unconscious in bed. It wasn't me—I was trying to drown myself anchoring the boat. Wasn't you, Sally; wasn't Weeks here—he was locked up."

"Wyatt—"

"Farley Wyatt's not the murdering kind. He had already won Nancy. He didn't give a damn if her old man approved or not; he was going to marry her and take her away."

"Cap wouldn't have had a reason."

"We'll get to that. Back to the sabotage. It was done by someone who knew just how to wreck things, someone who knew boats. This boat."

"He'd have to have a reason, Justice!"

"Oh, he did. Didn't you, Cap? He carried a grudge against Joe Jolly, and that extended itself to Jolly's woman. What did you say when Oakland asked you to sink her, Cap? What did he offer you anyway?"

Cap just caved in. His cherubic face looked a hundred years old suddenly. "He offered me my own boat. After he won the contract. Said there'd be plenty of boats running the river under his flag once he got the army contract. It didn't take much to convince me. Jolly took my boat from me. Jolly sunk the *Birmingham*!"

"That was an accident, Cap!"

"He sunk my boat! When I saw what he'd done, I made sure he'd go down with it."

"You killed Jolly!"

"Sure." Cap looked senile and childish at once. His blue eyes twinkled still but they were unfocused. "He sank my boat." Cap shrugged, asking for understanding. "I had to."

"Why the major?" Ruff asked. "Why kill him?"

"Do you know what that old bastard told me?" Cap grew angry again. "Told me he'd never seen a woman with so much guts. Said if she hadn't been sabotaged she would have run the *Nymph* off the river. Said as far as he was concerned, Sally had won."

"I thought the old hard-shell hated me," Sally said. "I thought he wanted me to lose!"

"I did too. He got drunk and told me that. No matter, he said, if you come in a day behind Oakland, he was going to see to it that you got the contract. Where did that leave me?"

"So you killed him."

"I hit him over the head. After he was dead, I made it look like an accident. Pretty clever." He chuckled, and Sally and Ruff looked at each other. "I always was pretty clever. Oakland knew that. Sally she just thought I was a charity case. She never knew how clever I was. Jolly knew, but Jolly had to pay the price . . ."

He went on for quite some time. After a while it didn't make any sense anymore. Sally called two sailors to take Cap MacAdoo below. There were tears in her eyes as she watched him go, his voice still rattling on.

"Lydell, you're pilot, I guess."

"Yes, Sally."

"Find Andy and tell him he's the new first mate."

"Yes, Sally."

Then there was no more conversation. Ruff inclined his head and Lt. Weeks followed him out.

"You heard all of it, didn't you?" Ruff asked the officer.

"Yes."

"You heard how the major wanted things to turn out. That he wanted Sally to have the contract. You also heard enough to realize what kind of character Oakland has. In fact, he's committed a lot of criminal acts trying to beat the *Jacksonville* upriver, somebody ought to think about having the bastard arrested."

"I'll tell them how it was," Weeks said. "That's why you took me along?"

"That's why."

Weeks watched the long river, listened to the chugging of the boat. "She's got the contract. When they hear my evidence, Oakland'll be lucky if he's not hung."

"Thanks."

"Don't thank me. It's what's right. If you'll excuse me, I've got to do something else that's right—make an apology. I hope they'll accept it."

"I think they will," Ruff said. Then he winked and Weeks grinned. The young officer walked off down the deck and Ruff watched him, thinking that maybe the kid was going to make it after all.

Sally came out on deck. She leaned beside Ruff, silent for a long while as the river slid past beneath the weary *Jacksonville.*

"I heard some of that, Ruff. Thank you."

"Just cut back your throttle and ease her in to Benton. You've won, you deserve it."

"Sure. I just wish it hadn't cost so damned much."

"Cap?"

She shook her head. There were still tears in her eyes. "Is he crazy?"

"Partly, I guess. His boat meant more to him than anything, more to him than people."

"Are you trying to tell me something, Mister Justice?"

Ruff smiled. "Would I, Sally?"

"Thanks." She kissed his cheek. "Guess what hard-shelled bastard finally got up the nerve to ask me to marry him?"

"Are you going to?"

She hesitated. "Yes. Yes, I think I am going to marry Lydell Cherry. What the hell, he likes me."

"And he's a good sailor."

"Yeah." She stuck out her tongue, kissed him lightly again, and said, "And so are you, Ruff Justice. If I had you long enough, I could probably make something out of you."

Then she went back to the wheelhouse. The tears were still there.

It was dark and low against the plains on the big bend in the river. Fort Benton was roughly made, roughly used. It looked vastly appealing just now, welcome after the long hard days and nights on the river. Ruff, Wyatt and Nancy, Weeks and Sally Shore stood at the forward rail, watching Benton grow larger. Now they could see individual men walking the parapets, see mules being led in through a side gate.

"There it is," Weeks said.

The *River Nymph* was tied up at the wharf and she was being unloaded by sailors and cavalry soldiers taking in welcome supplies for the post that had been cut off for so long by Red Cloud's armies.

"I'm glad I can't see the smirk on his face just now," Sally said.

"You wait. That expression will change when he gets the news that all of this was for nothing, and *that's* the expression I want to see."

They limped slowly toward the wharf, moving in opposite the *River Nymph*. The *Nymph* tooted her whistle derisively and Sally stiffened, muttering something about her shotgun.

"Just take it easy, Sally," Ruff said. "You've won. No point in losing our tempers now."

"No." She turned to watch Cherry steer the *Jacksonville* to its moorings. Taking a deep breath, she said, "You're right. I won't lose my temper."

"I mean it, Sally," Justice cautioned her.

"All right. Love thy enemy."

"That's the spirit."

He patted her shoulder and turned to watch the men unloading the *River Nymph*. As he did, he spotted Griff Oakland himself, standing on the wharf, staring back at Sally and Ruff.

"Love thy neighbor," Ruff said in a low voice.

Then Oakland turned his back and stuck his ass out at them, laughing contemptuously. Ruff was over the rail and across the wharf in three seconds. Oakland turned and tried to block the punch, but it didn't do him any good. Ruff caught him on the shelf of the jaw and the big man was knocked from the wharf and into the water where he floated sputtering and gasping while Ruff rubbed his knuckles.

Sally laughed loud and long—Ruff wasn't sure if it was directed at Oakland or at him. He waved his arm and started toward the fort, Weeks and Sally trailing after him. The first sergeant met them at the orderly-room door and invited him in.

"I'd like to speak to the commanding officer," Weeks said.

"So would I, sir," the burly first shirt said.

"He's not here?"

"Ain't been here for a week, sir."

"Who's in charge? Who's second in command?"

"Nobody's here. Just me. I'm ranking man, sir."

"You are!"

"That's right—or now Major Hawkins, I suppose. Is he with you?"

"Major Hawkins is dead."

"You're Lieutenant Weeks?" the sergeant asked.

"That's right."

"Then you're in charge, sir. It's your post, I guess."

"Damn." Weeks thought for a moment. "All right. First, get those goods back on the *River Nymph.* Don't brook any interference from Oakland. I'd arrest him if I was sure I had the authority. Then, Sergeant, you'd better tell me what your situation is here."

The sergeant, whose name was Conrad, did. Ruff, Sally, Weeks, and Sgt. Conrad sat in the commanding officer's office and Conrad told them what had happened.

"The captain—Captain Hall—went out to meet a

force of Cheyenne coming to Red Cloud's aid. This was a week ago. Our Crow scout came in and reported half a hundred Cheyenne warriors moving south to join the big army. Hall took a chance and went after the small band. Now he's cut off. I haven't got the people to go in after him, nor any way to get help."

Conrad told them, "I sent out three riders. None of them got through. The nearest help is Union, as you know, and there's no way anyone could get here for weeks, assuming they could make it through Red Cloud's area at all, which I doubt."

"The intelligence Hall received was no good?" Ruff Justice asked.

"No. Instead of fifty Cheyenne, he met a much larger force. This I got from a party of friendly Cheyenne drifting east, out of the war area. They say Hall is trapped"—he went to the wall map and pointed out the spot—"right here. His back to the river, two hundred Cheyenne and Sioux encircling him."

"Why are you here?" Sally asked. "Why aren't you trying to help him?"

"Ma'am, I've got seventy men including cooks and clerks. My orders from Captain Hall were to hold Fort Benton at all costs, to not let it fall into Red Cloud's hands. We've had five battles over the last three weeks with a major Sioux army. We've just about used up our ammunition. We've got sections of stockade wall that look like wormwood from the bullet holes. If things look peaceful today, believe me, it's all illusion. I was ordered to stay here, to hold the fort, and I will."

"I'm sorry," Sally said.

"It's all right. I just want you to understand now. Captain Hall is cut off, but there's not a damn thing I can do to help him. With Indians on three sides and his ammunition getting low as it must be, I'm afraid we've got the makings of another Little Big Horn up here."

"Not necessarily," Ruff Justice said.

"You have something in mind, Mister Justice."

"Yes, I do." Ruff went to the wall map as well, and he tapped it. "He's surrounded on three sides. Withdraw to the fourth."

"That's the river, Mister Justice!"

"Sure it is," Ruff answered. He looked at Sally Shore. "Sure it is."

"Do I understand you, Mister Justice? Use the steamboat to pull Captain Hall out of there? I couldn't order Miss Shore to risk her boat and her life."

"You wouldn't have to," Sally said.

"I couldn't even authorize it. I wouldn't dare."

"You won't have to do that either," Weeks said, speaking with some determination. "I'll take the responsiblity—if Miss Shore would risk it." Sally nodded. "Unless there is some other way we can hope to save the lives of Captain Hall and his men."

"Sir," Conrad said soberly, "there ain't no other way. But this way—it's a long shot too, ain't it?"

"It's a very long chance. It's also the only one we've got."

"Have you got a chaplain?" Ruff Justice asked.

The sergeant blinked at him in confusion for a minute. "Why, yes, Mister Justice," he stammered.

"Good. Tell him to put away his whiskey and find his Bible. We've got some young people that want to get married. Two couples, you tell him."

The sergeant glanced at Weeks, who nodded his approval. Ruff told Sally, "It'll make the trip downriver a hell of a lot more enjoyable for you and Cherry."

"Yeah, if we ever start back downriver. Thanks for volunteering me," Sally answered.

"You would have done it yourself."

"I was just about to. Will it work? Can we get them out of there, Ruff?"

"I don't know, but if we can't, Sally, no one can.

The chaplain will have a hell of a lot of work then, and it won't be a very cheering kind of work. All in all, I think he'd prefer weddings."

"All in all," said Sally Shore, "so would I."

15

The first sergeant was the one who had the idea. When Ruff and Sally emerged from the orderly room, they saw Griff Oakland being marched at rifle point to the guardhouse. Six of his men were with him.

"Those six," Sgt. Conrad said, "didn't think they ought to be helping out the US cavalry. The others on the *River Nymph* thought maybe they'd go along with us."

"You're taking both boats?"

"*You* are," Conrad answered. "You got two drivers—whatever you may call 'em?"

"I've got two. Have you got the authority to arrest Griff Oakland and take over his boat?"

"Nope. But I ain't gonna worry about that at this point, ma'am. They can take my stripes, but if I see Captain Hall and those damned lazy sons of bitches we call soldiers come in here alive and well, it'll be worth it."

"You won't lose your stripes," Weeks said. "I believe I might have ordered you to do this." He smiled at Ruff. "Let's get going. Time might mean something."

The word had already been passed to the steamboats. A head of steam was building in the *Jacksonville*'s boiler and in the *River Nymph*'s. Cherry was at the wheel of the *Nymph*, something that must have given him wry pleasure. The soldiers were loading wood as fast as they could, tearing apart everything that was loose.

"You've got finished lumber on board, don't you, Miss Shore?" Weeks asked.

"Yes, but that's army lumber, I wouldn't—"

"The army wants to use it now. Burn it if we need to."

Farley Wyatt showed up at the wharf with an army Springfield rifle.

Weeks shook his head. "You're not going."

"The hell I'm not! Is this going to start up again?"

"If you make it start up. You're not going. Don't tell me I can't order you around. Maybe not, but I can order these soldiers to keep you from coming aboard. I won't have Nancy widowed before she's married. Maybe she doesn't care for me, but I still care for her. Wyatt, you're not going!"

Farley and Nancy were on the shore watching as the boats pulled out fifteen minutes later, soldiers on their decks, smoke spewing darkly into the blue skies. Upriver was an Indian army and a beleaguered cavalry unit. It was a hell of a rescue party, but it was the only one available.

Ruff was on the *Jacksonville,* which, with Sally Shore at the wheel, led the way upriver. Weeks and the Indian scout found Justice on the forward deck.

"This is Sun Dog, Ruff. He's the scout who saw Hall's position. I thought it best he explain personally to you."

"Sun Dog," Ruff said, speaking the Crow tongue, "tell me what has happened to Captain Hall."

"Are you that one?" Sun Dog asked in surprise.

"What one do you mean?"

"The one who lived with Elk Tooth and took a Crow woman for a wife. The one the Crow call He-who-fights-our-enemies."

"I am that one," Ruff said. "Now tell me what has happened to Captain Hall."

Sun Dog did so, scratching a map in the deck of

the boat with the point of his knife, showing Ruff and Lt. Weeks the last position of the Sioux and Cheyenne army.

"Hall couldn't have moved from the river?"

"No," Sun Dog answered. "Even then they had made that impossible. He can go nowhere but into the water or to his grave."

"Yes. How many Sioux and Cheyenne are there, Sun Dog?"

"Too many."

The Crow looked up. Sunlight glinted on the silver ornaments he wore around his neck and in his hair. He told Ruff Justice, "Maybe a thousand. Maybe a thousand and half again."

Nobody heard the sharp word Ruff Justice breathed. He looked up to the wheelhouse, where Sally Shore steered the steamboat upriver. He had gotten her into this, gotten all of them into it. It was a long gamble and he was gambling with human lives. A thousand Sioux and Cheyenne, and they had a dozen soldiers, two dozen sailors. It was a very long gamble.

Ruff climbed up top and stood beside Sally, squinting upriver. The sun was a mirror off the surface of the wide Missouri.

"How far?"

"Not long now," Ruff answered. "You don't have to go through with this, Sally."

She laughed. "What's the matter, that Indian scout scare you?"

"That's right."

"Don't worry about me. I'm under army contract. This is all part of the service."

"Sure. If you weren't an engaged woman, I'd kiss you."

"I don't think Lydell will miss one," she said, turning her face toward his, her eyes misting.

Ruff placed one finger beneath her chin then and kissed her lightly, tasting her lips for the last time.

He broke away then, squeezing her shoulder. "You're all right, Sally Shore. You're a lot of woman."

"How far now?" she asked hoarsely, and turned her head sharply away.

"Around the big bend. I'll tell Weeks to get his soldiers ready."

Weeks had them ready. The cavalrymen stood at the rails licking dry lips, staring ahead, scratching nervously. One man crossed himself.

They rounded the big bend and simultaneously heard the rapid crackling of shots, like a string of firecrackers on the Fourth. Smoke rose in tiny puffs from behind the screen of brown willows that lined the river. Along the deck the weapons of sailors and soldiers were cocked. Ruff Justice checked his big .56 Spencer out, wondering as he did how much good it was going to do him.

The Crow had said a thousand Sioux. They wouldn't all be attacking a small force like Hall's, though, or Hall would already have been overrun. The main Sioux and Cheyenne camp was some five miles to the north, where the army of Red Cloud continued to mass.

They rounded the bend in the river and the gunfire began to sound more like what it was—death propelled by black powder.

"There they are!" Weeks shouted, and now they all could see Hall. His position was on a narrow spit of land protruding into the river. Before him was an open field of fire where they could see dead Indians and horses. The attack they had been listening to was breaking off. The Indians withdrew to the shelter of the willows onshore.

"They can't get the stubborn bastard out of there."

"He can't have much ammunition left."

Ruff had never met Captain Hall, but he felt admiration for the man. Cut off, he had found the only defensible position. Besieged, he had held out for days. He had nerve, but he seemed to have kept a cool head as well.

"We can't get in too close. Dammit, we'll have them swarming over us."

"How deep's the water?"

"Fifteen feet."

"Just so the horses have to swim," Ruff said. He shouted to Sally, "No nearer!"

"They'll have to swim," Weeks objected.

"That's right." He cupped his hands to his mouth again. "Hit that whistle, Sally." He looked down the line of armed men on the deck of the *Jacksonville*. "Make 'em count, boys."

The whistle blasted three times. They saw movement on the shore. A painted Sioux stood up behind the screen of willows and pointed. Ruff Justice shot him with the .56. It was a hell of a long shot but that gun was made for long-range flat shooting, for taking a buffalo down at distance, and Ruff had used that particular weapon some.

His shot set off a chain reaction of events. Other guns along the deck echoed his. A cheer, wind twisted, faint, sounded from the cavalry position. Sally's whistle bleated again and on the deck men shouted waving their arms at Hall's men.

"Come on! Come one, damn you!"

On their own or at a command from Hall, the soldiers on the shore dived for the water, some stripping off their shirts as they ran, throwing useless weapons aside.

A blood-chilling ululating cry went up from the willows. Half a hundred Sioux and Cheyenne, on horses and afoot, surged forward as the cavalry made its hasty retreat.

Guns spoke from the *Jacksonville* and from the *River Nymph,* which Cherry had put in close astern. Through the veil of smoke Ruff saw one of his shots tag a Sioux's war pony in the chest, saw the animal fold up and throw its rider.

A cavalryman died on the shore without having reached the river. Another was dragged between two comrades. The guns from the steamboats continued to lay down covering fire, but they couldn't hold back the onslaught of Sioux and Cheyenne braves for long.

The Indians were at the shore, firing, and then into the water on horseback, the warriors firing their new lever-action repeaters as they urged their war ponies on, swimming them toward the boat.

They made decent targets.

Ruff fired until his magazine was empty, and he reloaded hastily. A cavalryman, the second to reach the *Jacksonville,* reached up, gripped the rail, and was shot away by a Cheyenne. His mouth opened in silent plea, filled with blood, and he slid back into the water.

Justice fired three shots and tagged three braves. The Sioux must have had a lot of faith yet in Red Cloud's magic—they kept coming, knowing they were within easy range of the soldiers' bullets.

The man who appeared beside Ruff Justice was dripping water from his blue uniform. He had a craggy face, dark hair, a hawk's nose, black eyes. He wore two silver bars on the shoulders of his torn and bloodied uniform shirt.

"Using that Colt?" Capt. Hall asked.

Ruff slapped the butt of his revolver into the officer's hand and watched as Hall proceeded to empty it methodically and effectively into the approaching Indian army.

It was no way to fight a battle. The Indians' enthusiasm had prompted them to swim their ponies toward the boats instead of fighting from shore. They made easy targets, and despite the Sioux's overwhelming numerical superiority, they hadn't a chance.

"Get us out of here, Sally," Ruff shouted, only then seeing the dozens of bullet holes that peppered the walls of the wheelhouse.

She nodded, lifted her thumb, and engaged the paddle wheel. Slowly the ponderous *Jacksonville* turned as the fighting went on. The dead floated in the water, white and Indian. A painted war pony drifted to the *Jacksonville* and nudged it with its dead haunch.

The soldiers fired at anything that moved, while onshore the Indians ran along the bank, returning fire. The *Jacksonville* found her speed and drifted farther out into the middle of the wide river, the *Nymph* close behind her.

Sally tooted the whistle again and the *Nymph* answered in kind. There were still a few shots, but the sounds the guns made seemed far distant, otherworldly. And the *Jacksonville* steamed on, white smoke puffing from her ornate iron stacks, her stern wheel throwing up quicksilver curlicues.

"Captain Tyler Hall," the officer said. He stuck out his hand to Ruff Justice and gave him back the borrowed pistol. "Who do I thank for all of this?"

"The lady's name is Sally Shore. She's going to be running army freight up the river."

Hall looked to the wheelhouse, squinting into the sun. He nodded and then saluted. Sally tossed back a little salute of her own.

"Captain Hall?" Weeks saluted more formally and introduced himself.

"Is Major Hawkins with you?"

"Major Hawkins died, sir, en route."

"Sorry." Hall shook his head, genuinely sorry for the passing of a man he had never met. "That makes you commander of Fort Benton, Lieutenant Weeks."

"Me, sir?"

"You. I'm three weeks overdue for retirement. If you think that after today, after these last weeks, I'm going to wait for Washington to authorize regiment to send me another replacement, you are sadly mistaken. I know good fortune when I see it, and I do not intend to tempt fate any longer. I leave you with my best wishes and with Sergeant Conrad, who knows all there is to know about the subtler workings of the army, its paperwork, and the many loopholes avilable to a wise commander."

Hall wiped back his hair and looked upriver. He shook his head, and Ruff knew what was going on inside the man—the swelling of the heart, the elation, the heightened awareness of the five senses that had thought they were about to be extinguished.

"Anything else I can do for you, Lieutenant Weeks?"

"No, sir," Weeks stammered. "Ruff?"

Both men looked at Justice. Hall's eyes brightened. "I've got you placed now. Ruff Justice, is it? Yes, I've heard." He grinned then and clapped Ruff on the shoulder. "What do you say, Mister Justice—anything I can do for your men?"

"There's a matter of a couple of necessary and probably illegal steps we had to take to get this boat upriver, and the other boat. A man named Griff Oakland was arrested without proper authority. His boat was commandeered."

"We'll straighten all of that up, don't worry. I've never knowingly filed a false report, but if I have to do it for this last one, I will. We were dead, Justice, all of us." He looked at his wounded, half-drowned men who covered the deck of the steamboat. "We were counting the hours, the minutes. You tell me all about what's happened, about this Oakland, and we'll straighten it out."

They sailed on. The day was bright, the sky dotted with a few steam-white clouds. Ruff helped move the wounded soldiers into the cabins and then went up on deck again to watch the day pass away. He put his back against the sun-warmed cabin wall and then sank down to sit there, his eyes half-closed, soaking up the warmth of the day. That was where Lt. Weeks found him.

The young officer sat down beside Ruff.

Justice peered at him with one eye. "Everything straightened out?"

"I think so. Finally."

"Good."

"I mean all of it, Justice. Thanks to you. I've changed so rapidly in the past few days that I can't believe it. I see myself a lot more clearly, see what a fool I was making of myself, what a slavish idiot."

"Well, we all grow."

"Slowly sometimes. I can't even understand the man I was a little while ago, fawning over Hawkins when I knew he wasn't much of a soldier, much of a man. Look at Hall, there's a good officer. Worse, I kept trying to press myself on Nancy when a man with any sense at all would realize she didn't care for me."

"We all get a little blind," Justice said. "We run a single track. It's hard to switch, hard to get a good look at ourselves."

"You're generous," Weeks said.

"Why? Because I'm not willing to count you off? Weeks, you've got stuff in you, down deep. I know you do, and you've proven it today. The army needs you. I hope you're not going to resign that commission. I hope you'll stay on at Benton and do a job Captain Hall would be proud of."

They were rounding the big bend in the river now, and they rose to watch as Fort Benton came into view. Benton—encircled, battered, but holding on.

"It's something like coming home," Weeks said with wonder, and Justice knew the kid would be all right.

The wounded were carried off and then the supplies were unloaded from the *Jacksonville*. There was some uncertainty as to what to do with the goods on board the *River Nymph*, and so they were stored in the warehouse as well until the adjutant general up at regiment could straighten things out.

Griff Oakland was howling mad when they brought him out of the army stockade and marched him to the *Jacksonville*.

"The United States marshal ought to be through Bismarck this month, Griff. You tell him your story, all right? Maybe he'll decide not to arrest you. Maybe he'll charge the army instead. Think so?"

What Oakland thought wasn't clear. Cursing, sputtering incoherently, he was dragged away. Ruff watched him go, feeling no sorrow, no pity. Men had died because of Oakland's greed.

"Well," Sally Shore said, "it's just about over, isn't it?"

"Over, hell," Ruff Justice answered. "It hasn't hardly begun, woman. There's some important business to take care of."

16

"*This* is important business to you?" Sally Shore growled.

"Sure." Ruff grinned at her.

She looked awkward in her dinner gown, which was as close as she had been able to come to a wedding dress. Her hands were squeezing the sap from the stems of the violets she held. Lydell Cherry was in the commanding officer's quarters as well, wearing a collar that looked ready to strangle him. His hair was slicked back, his face red.

"He looks ready to make a break for it," Ruff said. "If he tries, I'll tackle him. I'm giving the bride away, and I insist there be a taker."

"Very funny," Sally said, her voice parched and small. "I'm ready to bolt myself. You only think this is amusing because it's not happening to you."

"Very likely," Ruff agreed. He took her arm and held it.

Nancy Hawkins looked like a bride is supposed to look: she had brought her trousseau upriver with her at her father's insistence. Now she was wearing gown and veil to marry Farley Wyatt, who was pale, rigid. Lt. John Lewis Weeks was their best man.

"Shall we begin?" the post chaplain, a small, spectacled young man, asked.

"The sooner the better," Ruff Justice answered. He

dropped Sally's arm rather abruptly when she gave him an elbow in the ribs.

They started downriver at dusk. Benton faded away into distance and darkness, and the *Jackonsville*, her white running lights on, her engines repaired, steamed toward Lincoln and home.

That first night they used their new anchor early, put the lights out, and the boat slept on the river. Ruff Justice walked the decks, studying the deep puzzle of the many-starred sky, listening to the muttering of the river, the whispered words it made in the willows.

He watched the night and the river until he could no longer bear it and then, cursing, he went to bed.

They hit the rapids the next day. Shooting down them was much easier than climbing up them. Easier and a hell of a lot faster and still hazardous, but Sally knew the rapids now, knew where the anchor rock was, where the river curled back over unseen depressions in the bottom, where it shelved and sideslipped, where it was shallow.

That night was another night for star watching. Below, the newlyweds slept or romped or held each other quietly.

Ruff Justice, you're just about useless on this trip back, he complained to himself.

There was no pressure of time, no need to battle Oakland and the Indians, to find a new branch of the river, to struggle up the white-water gorge. The engineers put wood in the furnaces and the steamboat paddled on. It would have made a nice cruise for a batch of schoolmarms.

He decided suddenly.

Marching to the lower deck, he retrieved his gear including the big Spencer repeater. Removing the lantern from the cabin wall, he checked the coal oil in it and took that along. Then he walked to Sally and Cherry's cabin and knocked on the door.

He heard Lydell growl a complaint, and he smiled.

"Who is it?" Sally asked, shushing Cherry.

"Ruff Justice."

Cherry growled again. Whispery footsteps approached the cabin door and Sally, her red hair all a-tumble, peered out.

"What's the matter?" she asked, her eyes excited and bright in the starlight.

"Nothin' at all. I wanted to let you know I was takin' the dinghy."

"What do you mean?" Sally shook her head, not understanding. "What would you want the dinghy for?"

"Can I have it or not? I'd hate to swim back to Fort Lincoln."

She was confused and apparently hurt. Her eyes met his and searched them. Cherry growled again. Ruff didn't blame the man a bit.

"Take the dinghy if you want. Ruff . . ."

He put his finger to his lips and then touched it to her nose, turned, and walked away into the night shadows. She watched after him for a long while.

The dinghy was tied up at the stern rail. Ruff Justice put his gear inside, climbed the rail, and cast off, rowing downriver and toward the shore. Distantly, far distantly a tiny red light showed against the darkness. He started in that direction.

The little arm of the river meandered around some through the oaks, but Ruff knew his way; he had been there before.

He rowed on, whistling to himself, stretching his body forward, leaning far back as he stroked with the oars. The Spencer was between his feet and Jack Troll's shacktown was a mile farther on.

The river didn't need a man like Jack Troll; the world didn't.

"If I let you be, you'll do the same things over, Jack Troll," Ruff muttered in between strokes. "You'll hit Sally Shore's steamboats . . . maybe somebody else's . . . You'll kill again . . . take young women again." He stopped rowing and the boat drifted toward the dark shore. "Can't allow that, Jack Troll. The river's dirty while you run it. I'm hear to clean it up a bit."

It wasn't going to be easy, but it wasn't as rough as trying to get a living woman out of Troll's stockade—there you had to be careful who got hurt.

They had a lot of men in there, but Justice figured he had a weapon they couldn't fight. Simple and effective. He was going to handle Troll and his men like he had once handled a dilapidated barn full of rats. He glanced at the lantern he had taken from his cabin, then patted the waterproof pack of matches he carried with him.

Eliminating the barn had gotten rid of the rats. Ruff meant to eliminate Troll's rat hole.

He shipped his oars as the bow of the dinghy approached the dark shore and then touched ground. With his rifle and lantern in one hand, Ruff stepped into the shallow dark water and went up on the bank to crouch, the dingy's painter in hand, searching the shadowed oaks.

He heard and saw nothing. Quickly he tied the dinghy and crept on toward the river pirate's stronghold. He could see the stockade now, jagged and irregular against the sky. A man was on the parapet on this night, striding carefully along, rifle over his shoulder, playing soldier.

Ruff moved softly across the fallen oak leaves. The guard must have been sleeping under the trees, but he was awake now as he emerged from behind the tree to level his pistol at Ruff's belly.

"Who is that?" the guard asked.

"Earl," Justice replied.

"The hell you are—" It had happened. "I'm Earl!"

Ruff had used Earl's name in vain once too often. The river rat came a step nearer, the pistol still on Ruff's belt line. Justice had the Spencer in his hand.

He could have brought it up and fired as quickly as the sleepy man could have squeezed off with that Colt. That would have accomplished little—they both would be hit, and hit hard at that range. Also the night Ruff had planned would be canceled. He didn't want that.

"I know you," Earl said slowly, his lip peeling back in a broken-toothed smile. "You're that damned scout that took Troll's girlie from him."

"That's right."

"What are you doing here now?" Earl asked.

"Came to finish the job. Came to stomp on Jack Troll."

"You're crazy!" Earl laughed out loud. "But I'll tell you this, Troll's going to be pleased to see you, scout. Yes, sir, he'll be very pleased to see you. Put that rifle down. You know I'm not going to miss."

"All right." Ruff did so.

"Make sure you do it easy. What do you think, Mister Scout, think you've got a charmed life or something? Coming back here like this. You must be insane."

"Very likely," Ruff said mildly, straightening up. He still held the lantern.

"Why don't you just drop your Colt too, Mister Scout. You don't have any use for that."

The man was getting irritating. Earl continued to smile, riding high on a feeling of power. Ruff took his revolver out of his holster.

"Do that easy too, friend."

"All right." Ruff put it on the ground beside the Spencer repeater.

"Now step back, Mister Scout."

Ruff took a step back, watching as Earl with glittering eyes reached for the captured weapons.

The lantern sang through the air, and as it met skull bone, there was a sickening little crunching sound. Glass shattered and steel bent. Earl went down on his face and stayed there.

Ruff Justice hummed softly as he picked up his guns. He took Earl's along for good measure. Peering at the damaged lantern, he shook it to make sure he hadn't broken the seam and allowed the coal oil to leak out. He hadn't. It was all right, if very badly dented.

"Earl, my man, you have got a hard head," Ruff Justice said under his breath. Then he started on, still humming that little tune.

The breeze was off the river. Ruff could feel it on his cheek. He looked toward the stockade and nodded with satisfaction. There was a card game or a fight or a drinking contest going on in one of the small lean-to shacks. Men's voices, slurred, angry, rose intermittently to make obscene comments against the clean silence of the night.

Ruff worked his way into a small declivity that ran from the stockade to the river. Apparently it was a drainage ditch. Half-filled with tin cans and mattresses, used lumber, it was fetid with offal.

Justice went on toward the shack, now dragging a ripped, half-empty straw mattress with him. A rat scurried away from beneath his boots and splashed into the stagnant water farther along.

Humming still, Ruff climbed from the ditch and in a crouch moved behind the shack where the argument was going on. Taking handfuls of straw from the mattress, he placed them next to the wall of the lean-to, splashed a little coal oil from his lantern onto that, and reached for a match.

Striking it with his thumb, he watched as bright flame curled up. He touched the match to the coal oil and stepped back. Once he saw that it had caught well, he moved along, glancing toward the stockade, where the guard would soon see the fire.

Not too soon, Justice hoped.

The other shack on that side was for storage. What was inside Ruff never discovered. It didn't matter.

He stripped the ticking mattress of its straw and splashed the rest of his coal oil onto the shack.

Ruff struck another match and stepped back. Almost immediately a cry went up from the wall—the first fire had been spotted. Circling back toward the ditch, Justice ran into a choking river rat emerging from the lean-to. He clubbed him down with his rifle, half-tripped over the falling man, who clutched at his legs and ran on.

Someone shouted, "Fire. Goddammit, the shack's on fire. The stockade!"

The fire had already reached the stockade, and it was flaring up hotly, curling against the palings. Men rushed from the stockade with water buckets in hand. Ruff shot two of them and the rest rushed for cover. The fire roared on and soon there was nothing anyone could have done to stop it.

It dominated the night, reddening the sky, blotting out the stars, painting the river shifting golds and reds. The stockade was a wall of flame. The three flatboats moored at the wharf had caught fire. There was a fourth nearby just starting to go.

A river pirate with his shirt on fire, hands held high ran toward the river.

And then Ruff saw Troll.

Wearing only jeans and boots, the big man was running toward the flatboat, his hair in a wild tangle, his body smudged with soot. Behind Troll a section of the stockade collapsed as the rawhide ties were burned away. Troll's mouth opened in a furious roar. Whatever it was that he said, the crash of the collapsing stockade blotted it out.

Flames danced skyward in long lashing tongues. Sparks shot up against the night in golden fountains. Troll, backlighted by the hell Justice had devised, raised frenzied arms and cursed all of heaven and earth.

Troll turned then and started toward the river with the rest of his people. Men plunged into the black waters and swam for the opposite shore. Every building on Ruff's side of the river had caught fire now, save one distant outbuilding.

Ruff nodded with satisfaction. "That takes care of the barn," he said.

Troll had reached the river, but he had no intention of swimming. He leapt for the single flatboat that wasn't engulfed in flames, and landed heavily on its deck. He dragged himself toward the tiller, one ankle apparently sprained.

There was fire in the deckhouse, but it was burning slowly. Troll obviously hoped to put it out, to float downriver, to start again, to build a new and better fortress, to kill again.

Ruff started running toward him.

He moved swiftly, smoothly, the fire dancing around him, the wind lifting his long dark hair. He hit the wharf at a dead run and ran its length, leaping high and far to land on the deck of the flatboat which was under way now, creeping away from the inferno of the shore.

"Scout!" Troll bellowed, and with an awesome display of fury and strength he ripped the tiller from the flatboat. The handle shattered and Troll looked at it once, grinning—if the mad, animal expression could be called a grin—as he saw he had a perfect club, three feet long, solid oak. He meant to crush Ruff's skull with it, to pulp his brain.

Troll stalked forward. Behind him the eerie, firelit sky danced with color as if the air itself had caught flame.

"You took my wife, scout."

"She wasn't your wife, you maniac. You think any decent woman would even look at you, let alone marry you?"

Ruff backed off a bit. His rifle was held waist high. But Troll wasn't to be intimidated by fear of pain, fear of death. He was an animal, hardly aware of his own mortality. You can't frighten such men; you can only eliminate them.

"I had me a wife. Lots of wives. I got 'em all the time off the boats on the river."

"Then what happens to them?" Ruff backed off another step. "Where are they all now?"

"Dead," Troll said. His voice was low, his expression moronic. "They get bad, and so I have to put 'em down."

"Kill them?"

"When they're bad, when they won't mind me."

Ruff had come to the end of the deck. The flatboat fire, left alone, had built to a steady, hot blaze that was devouring the deckhouse. The heat was intense. Ruff's face was lighted by the fire. Sweat trickled down into his eyes.

"When they won't mind you—what does that mean?"

"I want 'em to do things for me. You can guess." The moronic face brightened with its dirty little secret.

Ruff didn't even want to guess what the tiny brain behind those tiny eyes could come up with in the way of sex. "So you kill them."

"I have to. Sooner or later. Then I get me a new one. I need a woman, Justice. And you took my new one from me." Troll came steadily forward, waving the broken tiller back and forth.

"I had to. She wanted to marry someone else—a human being."

Troll roared and leapt forward. Ruff's Spencer came up, but Troll's arcing club rang against it, slamming it from Ruff's hands. Troll struck again and the club grazed Ruff's temple, dazing him.

"I'm gonna kill you now, boy," Troll said.

Justice shook his head. He backed away, holding crossed forearms in front of his face. At his back the fire roared as the flatboat was engulfed by flames.

"Now I'm gonna kill you," Troll repeated. He marched onward, still swinging his club. Then he swung again, hard, his face alight with the flames and with savage glee.

Ruff ducked and kicked out. The club struck the burning deckhouse behind Ruff. Burned-through timbers collapsed and sparks flew. Ruff was having trouble breathing, trouble seeing in the smoke. He could see only Troll, shirtless, huge, savage, hovering over him.

Ruff saw the club go up again and he kicked out hard at Troll's shin, rolling away across the burning deck, his mind still fuzzy, his reactions still slow. Troll came at him again—a monstrous dark apparition against the flaming night.

"You took my wife," Troll growled. His voice was barely human. His hulking body trembled with his deep, baseless rage. He screamed and lifted the club once more.

The bowie was riding on Ruff's belt, and now his hand closed around the stag handle. Troll never saw the polished steel of that curved blade, the flame, liquid and bright, dancing on the mirror surface of it.

The club started down and Justice gathered one foot under him and drove upward with all of his strength, his shoulder joint popping with the strain as he drove the bowie deep into the river pirate's gut, tearing upward, ripping entrails and abdominal muscles before the tip of the knife struck heart and Troll gave one last savage bellow, staggered back, and flopped to the deck, his body leaking life.

Ruff tried to get up, tripped, and went down. He rose again and stood dazed, watching the night and the inferno. The flatboat was alive with writhing flame. There was no way out but through a wall of fire. Ruff put his arm over his face and leapt.

The world was intensely hot for a time. Ruff's nostrils filled with the scent of burning cloth and buckskin, of singed hair, and then he was plunged into a cold, dark vacuum that smothered the heat, the momentary pain.

When he bobbed to the surface, he was already fifty feet from the burning flatboat, which drifted downstream carrying Jack Troll's body like some ancient Viking funeral barge.

Ruff trod water for a long while, just his head above the dark river. The flatboat came apart then, breaking into two sections before one last hot sheet of flame destroyed it. A piece of planking lifted on end and then slid away beneath the surface of the river. In another minute there was nothing but the smell of fire. Then there was not even that, just the timeless river and the endless night.

Ruff Justice swam toward shore.

He found the dinghy where he had left it, untied it, and shoved off. There was still some smoke above the ruined river pirate's stronghold, but the flames were out, the town itself a heap of ash and rubble.

He got the boat turned and let it drift, steering with one oar. He lay his head back and watched the stars drift past. He hummed a soft, tuneless song as the river took him homeward. It was a long way to Fort Lincoln.

WESTWARD HO!

The following is the opening section from the next novel of the gun-blazing, action-packed new Ruff Justice series from Signet:

RUFF JUSTICE #19: FRENCHMAN'S PASS

It was a simple job, but it bothered Willard Tillits: find this man called Ruff Justice and put a bullet in his brain.

It was simple because everyone in Bismarck, Dakota Territory, knew the man and could tell you where he was. And Justice had never seen Tillits, never heard of him, so he had no reason to suspect that Willard would want to put a bullet in his brain.

That was on the plus side. The minus was that this Ruff Justice was the damnedest piece of work you ever saw. He spent most of his time squiring a certain lady around—a tall woman with Spanish blood and a body that would make a sculptor weep.

He did that, but this Ruff Justice had funny ideas of what you did with a woman. Willard Tillits had had his own women from time to time. Annie Gates, for instance, who was just fine once you got her off that bum leg . . . But this Ruff Justice was a piece of work. He had caught him, for instance, that one time up in the tree with this Spanish woman, and you had never seen anything like that.

Once, when Willard had been ready to put that .44 slug in his skull and earn the five hundred dollars he would get for putting it there, Justice had gotten up with that woman and started dancing, swirling all around in circles. In the oak grove. In the middle of the night. Naked.

So that was the kind of man this Ruff Justice was. How could you take him serious?

Even down in Missouri Willard Tillits had heard of this Ruffin T. Justice. He was rated pretty high by them that knew. Jack Craig had seen this Justice carve a man up with a bowie knife real bad. They said he was a big Indian fighter. But how could you take him serious?

A man that went walking around with his hair as fine and pretty as a lady's combed down across his shoulders. He had been wearing a ruffled shirt the other night and a dark suit with silver buttons—before he shed the whole crop to go naked and dance.

Another night Tillits had seen Justice with a rose in his hair. And this was a growed man who was supposed to be some kind of heller with a gun and a knife!

Tillits hadn't seen a sign of a sidearm, nor of the .56 Spencer repeater they said he toted. Nor was there a bowie knife hanging from him. Maybe there was a weapon up under his coat, in one of those fancy shoulder holsters—Tillits had his suspicions, but he hadn't actually seen it. Anyway, what kind of man wears a shoulder holster.

The voice was coming to Tillits through the trees. He shook his head again, wondering. You just couldn't take the man serious. Not even for five hundred dollars.

* * *

"Time weeps with shame at the few glad hours
It's spared for us my dear one
When it knows to love you endlessly
Is all I need for completion . . ."

What it was was poetry. A man out in the woods with a big-breasted Spanish woman in the middle of the night spouting poetry. Did that make sense?

Tillits listened for a while longer. It didn't get any better. He shook his head as if to shake the poetry out of his ears.

Once some newspaperman back East had found some writing of Ruff Justice's, something about the Battle of Crossed Lances, about the Indians charging and dying, the sweat and pain of the cavalry as they held them back, and this man—in Philadelphia, it was—had said how Justice was a frontier original, an *American* original, a Westerner, filled with the power of the wild, raw land. A lot of people had read that poem and they had made him some sort of celebrity so that Justice had toured with the Bill Cody show and read that poem in a lot of places, even in Europe.

The newspaperman must have been drunk.

Tillits crept nearer. He could see him now, see his bare back. He was sitting on a fallen log, looking out across the broad, dark Missouri River. The woman was beside him, her hair down—it was nearly as long as Justice's—her head on his shoulder, her back as bare as his.

Justice had temporarily left off the poetry. His hand was doing something between the woman's thighs. Tillits found that idea very stimulating, but he hadn't come for that. He'd come to put a bullet in the crazy bastard's head and get his five hundred dollars and get out of Bismarck.

"It feels so good," she was saying. "A little

higher. Along that little ridge. Oh, God, that's good. Yes."

She held his hand with her own and closed her eyes in ecstasy. They could hear the river flowing past, muttering muted words. Upriver a steamboat whistled although it was nearly ten o'clock. No other sounds drifted to them here in the silent grove. There was only the night and Ruff Justice, and Carmen opened her eyes, turning to him, her lips parting, tugging him down to her, this wild and strong and unpredictable man.

"Do me, Ruffin Justice. Again, please do me. You know the way I like it."

Ruff Justice considered himself a gentleman. Others may have had different opinions, but they didn't know him as intimately as Ruff knew himself. At any rate, he was gentleman enough to do as the lady requested without quibbling.

He rolled her over and down, off the log and onto the soft, dew-moistened grass where Carmen, with heated breath, with her lips parted to reveal her fine white teeth, with her dark eyes shining expectantly, opened her knees to him.

"Let me see," Ruff said, "was this the way you liked it?"

"Any way."

"Or"—he kissed her—"the other?"

"Any, so long as it is quick," Carmen said, and she pulled him down, her mouth crushing itself against his. And it would have been quick, very quick, but for a man from Missouri named Willard Tillits.

Carmen wound Ruff's long dark hair around her fingers and she sighed, staring at him with pleasured eyes. "You are a good one, a good man . . ."

Her eyes opened even wider suddenly and she pushed at Ruff, her fingers clawing at him.

"There, Ruffin!"

Ruff rolled away. With the instincts of a plainsman he moved at the first hint of a threat, diving toward the Colt New Line .41 pistol that sat in its shoulder holster next to his coat.

He had his hand on the Colt when the pistol from the woods barked. The bullet missed Ruff, spattered Carmen with earth and leaf litter. She screamed in anger and frustration more than in fear.

Ruff, the Colt in his hand, rolled over the log he had been sitting on and dashed for the woods. Another shot followed him, missing his bare heel by inches.

Willard Tillits cursed. Slowly, profusely cursed. He had missed and now he had that crazy man loose in the oaks with a gun in his hand.

The woman, naked and as mad as a wet hen, was sitting on the ground, pounding it with her fists and heels as she ranted away in Spanish. Tillits didn't care about the woman except to notice how she was built.

He started to withdraw, knowing he had a cougar in the oak grove. Justice hadn't seemed like much, but he had moved very quickly. He had known where his gun was at all times, known which way he was going to go if there was trouble . . . and now you couldn't hear the bastard.

He was like a big cat or an Indian. Silent.

Unless Justice was lying out there dead or scared, not moving a muscle, then he was as silent as a cougar, silent as death.

Tillits started to ease away, to move back toward his horse, which was tethered on the other side of the little oxbow. Upriver the steamboat whistle sounded again.

Tillits started on. The arm of a giant oak tree reached across the path toward him and Tillits nearly fired his gun in panic. Looking back, he hurried toward the oxbow.

He didn't know why he was suddenly afraid, but he was. He had discounted the stories about Justice until now. Seeing him strutting around town, you could hardly credit the tales you heard.

It had seemed easy—a bullet in the brain. Five hundred dollars.

Tillits had killed a lot of men, and once a woman. All for money. Nothing had ever gone wrong. They didn't know him from Adam, and so it was easy. You just waited and then found them alone or vulnerable. You just sidled up beside them and put a bullet in their brain. And then you were paid.

Tillits tripped over a root and went down in a pile of leaves and sticks. It sounded like a crashing door. He rose again and hurried on. Justice was back there—no matter. There would be another chance, another time if only Tillits could get out of the oak grove, get to his horse.

And then he saw his horse—across the oxbow where he had tied it. With relief Tillits started wading the river, wading it as quickly as the hip-high water allowed. The horse watched his approach. Frogs grumbled and croaked in the cattails downstream. The big Missouri flowed past beyond the trees. The stars were huge and silver.

Ruff Justice was there on the shore.

Ruff Justice was there and Tillits felt his heart leap into his throat. He had his pistol in his hand and he lifted it to shoot the naked man. If he could just get a bullet into him, he could take a year off, maybe longer. He could shack up with big Annie Gates and drink whiskey all day and all night.

He jerked his pistol up, but it was too late. He knew already that it was too late. As he tried to squeeze the trigger, he saw the red flower blossom at the muzzle of Justice's Colt, saw the recoil lift Justice's arm, saw the puff of black-powder smoke.

And then—oh, God!—the mule kicked him square in the middle of the chest and the fiery spasm of pain erupted inside his chest. He still had the pistol in his hand, but it was useless. It was so damned heavy no one could lift it and fire it. He would never buy a gun that heavy again. They weren't worth a damn. People could just shoot you and you couldn't lift your goddamn gun.

Tillits saw that the smoke was clearing, drifting away in the wind so that the haze in front of the brilliant, close stars was gone. It was gone and then it came back. Blood-red and liquid.

"I think . . ." Willard Tillits began, but no one would ever knew what he thought. It was incomplete, an impulse the brain had begun to deliver to the uncaring universe before the dark time came and the thought, small and insignificant, was snuffed out by death.

Willard Tillits slumped into the water and, face-down, floated away down the oxbow toward the wide, dark Missouri beyond the big oaks.

On the shore the tall man watched. He was naked, long-haired, and pretty well aggravated. The body of a man he had never even known went floating past and Ruff Justice watched. It wasn't a gratifying sight.

With his gun dangling from his hand, he watched until what had been Willard Tillits was around the river bend and out of sight. Then he turned and walked to the man's horse.

It was folded up in the saddlebags. Inside a tobacco tin.

> It will be five hundred if you put a bullit through Ruff Justice. He is apt to be verry much in our way. Know you'll do this as you have always done good work in the past.
>
> P.S.—Best time with this one is probly when he is sleeping with some woman, which is most of the time it seems.

* * *

It wasn't signed. Ruff tossed the note down. He looked to the silent river again and then went back to what he seemed to be doing most of the time: which was sleeping with some woman.

And Willard Tillits went sailing away toward the Gulf of Mexico a thousand miles away.

JOIN THE *RUFF JUSTICE* READERS' PANEL

Help us bring you more of the books you like by filling out this survey and mailing it in today.

1. Book Title: ______________________________

   Book #: ____________

2. Using the scale below, how would you rate this book on the following features? Please write in one rating from 0-10 for each feature in the spaces provided.

POOR		NOT SO GOOD			O.K.		GOOD		EXCEL-LENT	
0	1	2	3	4	5	6	7	8	9	10

	RATING
Overall opinion of book	______
Plot/Story	______
Setting/Location	______
Writing Style	______
Character Development	______
Conclusion/Ending	______
Scene on Front Cover	______

3. About how many western books do you buy for yourself each month? ____________

4. How would you classify yourself as a reader of westerns?
   I am a ( ) light ( ) medium ( ) heavy reader.

5. What is your education?
   ( ) High School (or less) ( ) 4 yrs. college
   ( ) 2 yrs. college ( ) Post Graduate

6. Age ________ 7. Sex: ( ) Male ( ) Female

Please Print Name______________________________

Address______________________________

City ______________ State ____________ Zip ____________

Phone # ( )____________

Thank you. Please send to New American Library, Research Dept., 1633 Broadway, New York, NY 10019.